"I've been drinking your wine all evening, so I really shouldn't drive home."

Paige withdrew and gave him a hard look. "Is that the only reason you're staying?" she demanded with mock severity.

His smile became a grin before he pulled her close and kissed her. "You must learn to trust me, Paige," he chided her at last. "I'm going to stay because I need to hold you, just hold you close for a very long time."

"And is that all you're going to do, just hold me?"

Grant's smile deepened. "We'll start with holding and see where it goes from there."

"Then turn out the light, Grant," she invited. "I think it's time for bed."

Elizabeth N. Kary *worked for twelve years as an art teacher in rural upper New York state. During that time she began work on* Love, Honor and Betray, *a historical novel set during the War of 1812 which Berkley will publish in January 1986. Elizabeth now lives with her husband in St. Louis, Missouri, where she works part-time with children's art classes.*

Dear Reader:

The August books are here—and what a terrific bunch they are!

In *Such Rough Splendor* (#280), Cinda Richards—who delighted us with her zany *This Side of Paradise* (#237)—has penned a romance that we think will become a classic of the genre. The best elements of romance come together with superlative skill in this warm, funny, poignant tale of love and healing, as divorcée Amelia Taylor makes war and peace with, in her words, "the biggest, dumbest cow puncher she's ever clapped eyes on." Houston "Mac" McDade will live on in your memories as one of the most original and irresistible heroes you've ever had the good fortune to lock horns with!

Sarah Crewe explores the complexities of pursuit and revenge in *Windflame* (#281), a strong follow-up to her earlier romances. Melissa Markham's job as college fundraiser forces her to pursue wealthy Dakin Quarry for his money, but her immediate attraction to him vastly complicates the situation. Distrust, scandal, revenge, and Dakin's own fatal passion for Melissa combine to form a compelling, tension-filled love story set against a quiet college campus.

Lauren Fox's zest-filled, lusty romance *Storm and Starlight* (#282) will catch you up and whirl you away—just as Eric Nielson does to Maggie McGuire when she arrives to investigate the proposed expansion of his satellite-dish manufacturing company. There's never a dull moment as Maggie struggles to curb Eric's exuberant excesses and Eric gets Maggie into one outrageous situation after another. The banter flies fast and furious and the action's nonstop as these two forceful characters love and live with passionate energy.

In *Heart of the Hunter* (#283), Liz Grady has outdone herself, creating Mitch Cutter, a hard-boiled, gun-slinging bounty hunter who fears nothing except love, and Leigh Bramwell, a dyed-in-the-wool romantic with a long streak of cowardice. Never has a man so inept with "nice girls"—a man whose only way of loving a woman is by deceiving and possessing her—seemed so heart-wrenchingly appealing. *Heart of the Hunter* is a romance you'll read with excitement—and cherish for years to come.

Lucky's Woman (#284) will tug at your heartstrings and make you smile through your tears as only a romance by Delaney Devers can. With roughhewn "Lucky" Verret and ladylike Summer Jordan, Delaney creates a love so potent it has the power to destroy the very hearts it fills. You'll shiver with Summer as she braves mosquitoes, mud-creatures, and mayhem in the Louisiana swamp she loathes, in order to prove her loyalty to stubborn-as-sin Lucky. You'll ache with Lucky as he hides his longing from the woman he secretly cherishes but fears he cannot trust. All of you who raved about Delaney's *The Heart Victorious* (TO HAVE AND TO HOLD #40) and asked for more will find *Lucky's Woman* just the treat you've been waiting for.

Finally, SECOND CHANCE AT LOVE is pleased and proud to introduce a stunning new talent—Elizabeth N. Kary, author of *Portrait of a Lady* (#285). Here is an adult romance in the best sense of the word, the story of two complex characters whose struggles to trust and understand each other lead to an intimacy that's deep and powerfully satisfying. The maturity of Elizabeth's characters, the elegance of her writing style, and the page-turning quality of her story all set *Portrait of a Lady* apart as truly special. Don't miss the debut of this wonderful writer—and don't miss her first historical romance, *Love, Honor and Betray*, to be published by Berkley in January. This epic adventure and passionate love story set during the War of 1812 is destined to establish Elizabeth N. Kary as a romance writer of stature!

Enjoy these August romances and please keep your letters and questionnaires coming. We love reading them.

Best,

Ellen Edwards

Ellen Edwards, Senior Editor
SECOND CHANCE AT LOVE
The Berkley Publishing Group
200 Madison Avenue
New York, NY 10016

PORTRAIT OF A LADY
ELIZABETH N. KARY

A SECOND CHANCE AT LOVE BOOK

PORTRAIT OF A LADY

Copyright © 1985 by Elizabeth N. Kary

All rights reserved. No part of this publication may be reproduced or transmitted in any form or by any means, electronic or mechanical, including photocopy, or any information storage and retrieval system, without permission in writing from the publisher.

Requests for permission to make copies of any part of the work should be mailed to: Permissions, Second Chance at Love, The Berkley Publishing Group, 200 Madison Avenue, New York, NY 10016.

First edition published August 1985

First printing

"Second Chance at Love" and the butterfly emblem are trademarks belonging to Jove Publications, Inc.

Printed in the United States of America

Second Chance at Love books are published by
The Berkley Publishing Group
200 Madison Avenue, New York, NY 10016

To Joan Bramsch,
without whose encouragement
and prodding this venture
into contemporary fiction
would never have been undertaken.

CHAPTER
One

"WHAT THE HELL is this all about?" demanded the blue-eyed giant who loomed in the doorway of the Conservation Department of the Tri-City Art Museum. "What's this foolishness about 'The Lady of Dordrect' being a forgery?"

Paige Fenton rose abruptly to her feet, ready to defend her allegations, a flush of indignation rising in her cheeks and a crackle of unexpected physical response to the man licking through her.

But before she could answer, Arthur Franklin, the museum's director, stepped forward. "Mr. Hamilton, I'm so glad you could come right over."

"This had better be as serious as you claimed, Franklin. It caused the cancellation of an important business meeting," Hamilton growled.

"I assure you, I wouldn't disturb you if there was any question about our findings."

In spite of Franklin's calming manner, the newcomer's anger was evident to Paige in the rigid set of his broad shoulders and the harsh lines that marred his handsome face.

"All right, Mr. Franklin, let's not waste time with empty assurances. I want to know why you believe the painting the Hamilton Corporation sold you is a fake and who is responsible for these ridiculous accusations."

Turning to Paige, Franklin made the necessary introductions: associate conservator to infuriated patron.

Though Paige had steeled herself for this confrontation with the portrait's former owner, she was unprepared for the open hostility in Grant Hamilton's sapphire-bright eyes. She bristled as she felt them sweep over her, taking in her severe auburn topknot, huge tortoise-shell glasses, and conservative dark clothes visible where her lab coat hung open. That his gaze was measuring, calculating, and at the same time contemptuous fueled the instantaneous dislike she felt for him. Determined not to be intimidated either by his sun-drenched good looks or the derisive gleam in his eyes, she stared back with equal intensity, noting the faded plaid shirt and well-washed jeans that clung to his muscular body like a second skin. Judging from his rugged build and rough demeanor she decided he looked far more like the tight end for the local football team than a patron of the arts.

"Well then, tell me, Miss Fenton, how did you come to the mistaken conclusion that the Hals my company sold the museum is a forgery?" There was such blatant condescension in the visitor's tone that a sharp retort bubbled to Paige's lips. But Arthur Franklin forestalled it.

"Please, Mr. Hamilton, let's sit down and discuss this rationally," he offered.

"Perhaps, Arthur, if I could show Mr. Hamilton what I found while I was cleaning the portrait," Paige suggested coldly, "he might be more inclined to believe what we say."

She'd issued a challenge, and Grant Hamilton rose to

meet it, the hint of a sneer in his smile. "Very well, Miss Fenton, let's see what you've discovered."

Paige led the way across the studio to where the portrait lay on one of the worktables. It was a truly breathtaking piece, allegedly painted by Frans Hals, the old Dutch master, who had practiced his art in Haarlem during the mid-seventeenth century. The portrait, known as "The Lady of Dordrect," was of a young Burgher woman and had been carefully painted to reveal her pale beauty above severe dark clothes and beneath a prim Brussel's lace cap. It was as fine an example of Hals's technique as Paige had ever seen, rich with character and vibrant with quick, clean brushstrokes that typified the artist's work.

Adopting her best lecture-hall voice, Paige began to explain. "Before I decided on any kind of restoration for the portrait, I made a careful examination of the painting to determine its condition. The work was in excellent shape, due, I thought, to the care the Hamilton family has always taken with its acquisitions. At any rate, the only conservation necessary at this time was the removal of a protective overcoating of darkened varnish and its replacement with one of the new non-yellowing polymers."

"As fascinating as all this is," Grant Hamilton observed caustically, "what does it have to do with determining that 'The Lady' is a forgery?"

"As I began to remove the varnish," Paige continued, ignoring the provocation in his tone and the tremors of reaction that raced along her limbs, "I became suspicious of the painting's origins. In testing for the correct solvent to remove the overcoating, I realized the varnish was of a modern formula. That in itself is not unusual since paintings of this age have often been cleaned and resealed several times, but as I used the solvent I'd decided on, it became evident that a toner of some sort had been used to give the painting a patina of great age. Also, the pigments beneath the tinted overcoating were too strong and fresh to have been applied more than three hundred years ago."

Grant Hamilton looked plainly unconvinced as he turned to the museum director. "Do you mean to tell me the accusation that 'The Lady of Dordrect' is a forgery is based solely on this woman's subjective judgment?"

Anger rocketed through Paige, and she glared at him.

"You must understand," Franklin defended her, "that a great deal in the art world is based on subjective judgment. But in this case our experts concur with Paige. I would never have contacted you if we weren't convinced that this work is not all it seems."

Bless you, Arthur, Paige commended him silently as she beamed at the dapper little man, who handled the complex operations of a nationally known museum with great tact and aplomb.

"Of course, Mr. Hamilton," Paige added, "there are a number of scientific tests that we will run on the portrait now that a question of its authenticity has arisen. Perhaps you will find those objective results more convincing than my evaluation. Either way, the findings will be the same: 'The Lady of Dordrect' is a forgery."

Grant Hamilton's face hardened at the quiet arrogance in her words, and a flare of mistrust passed between them.

Then he gave a feral smile. "You may be right, Miss Fenton, but be assured that if 'The Lady of Dordrect' is authentic and you are wrong, I intend to see to it that you resign your position."

Turning to the museum's director, he continued, "Tell me, Mr. Franklin, how is it possible that when we had the painting examined at Riverview prior to the sale, no question of its authenticity was raised? And what about the picture's documentation, which dates back a full one hundred years before my great-grandfather acquired the piece? Is all that invalid if this portrait turns out not to be by Hals?"

"Those are all good questions, Mr. Hamilton, and I'm not sure how to answer you," Franklin conceded. "Unfortunately, Mr. Argenta, the man who examined the work at

Portrait of a Lady

your brother's estate, is out of the country at present, though we are trying to contact him.

"I'm sure you realize how important it is that we resolve these questions quickly," Franklin went on. "The Northern Light exhibition, featuring both Dutch and Flemish painters of this period, is due to open in just a week, and publicity has already begun. Since we're using 'The Lady of Dordrect' as a signature piece for the show, both the museum and Hamilton Corporation will suffer great embarrassment if the portrait proves to be a fake."

Grant Hamilton's expression was grave. "Does this discovery jeopardize the authenticity of the other pieces included with the purchase of the Hals?"

Paige could see that Arthur Franklin felt uncomfortable with the question and its ramifications. "It seems to me that the museum would be negligent if we didn't run a few basic tests on the other pieces, especially considering the huge sums of money involved."

Hamilton stiffened. "Then you're insinuating that someone has attempted to defraud you."

The usually self-possessed Arthur Franklin fumbled for a reply. "That conclusion seems premature, Mr. Hamilton. We really don't know enough about the forgery yet to assign blame."

The younger man took a deep breath. "Then get those damned tests done! I want to know where Hamilton Corporation and I stand in all this." His narrowed eyes swept up from the portrait to the museum director and came to rest on Paige. In these past few minutes they had become enemies, and she felt his antagonism keenly.

Still, Paige managed to stare back, determined not to be bullied by either this man's intimidating physical presence or his family's power.

Arthur Franklin broke the uncomfortable silence. "Rest assured, Mr. Hamilton, we'll be running those tests as soon as possible. The museum is as anxious as you are to get to the bottom of this unfortunate incident. Now, why don't you let me show you out?"

"No, thank you, Franklin. I can find my own way," Hamilton said stiffly, and he slammed the door behind him as he left.

After Grant Hamilton's thunderous exit Paige retreated to one of the huge leather wing chairs in the lab's windowed alcove to regain her composure. The encounter with the portrait's former owner had deeply upset her. That a man like Grant Hamilton, who obviously knew nothing about art, could question her judgment and threaten her job enraged and frightened her.

She was very much aware of the power money could wield at an institution that existed primarily on bequests and private or corporate gifts. Nor did she underestimate the importance of the Hamilton family in providing, both directly and indirectly, for Tri-City's small but impressive collection of art.

Because of his family's influence, Paige knew that, should Grant Hamilton demand her head on a Paul Revere platter, Arthur Franklin would be forced to comply. It wasn't a comforting thought, but she didn't dwell on it. After all, she was right; the Hals was a forgery. By Monday the tests would be completed and her suspicions confirmed. Then Grant Hamilton would be forced to acquiesce.

Paige was still feeling smug an hour later as she piloted her temperamental Toyota toward her apartment in a newly rehabilitated area to the west of the museum. Once home, she turned up the air conditioner and stripped off her clothes in preparation for a shower. Arthur Franklin was hosting another fund raiser tonight, and Paige knew he expected her to attend. Actually, contemplating victory in her confrontation with the overbearing Grant Hamilton had put her in a fine mood, and she was looking forward to the party.

Paige wasn't sure why she had taken such an instantaneous dislike to Hamilton; she had disagreed with patrons

Portrait of a Lady

before without feeling such animosity toward them. Perhaps it had been his arrogant manner or her long-standing belief that no man that good-looking could be trusted.

Picking up a sketch pad from her bedside table, she indicated a broad jaw and square chin with a few swipes of her pencil. A vertical line became a straight, narrow nose, while horizontal strokes formed a full, sensuous mouth. Shading in high cheekbones and heavy brows above wide-spaced eyes, she conceded that she had captured a fair likeness of her handsome adversary. She tossed the pad aside in irritation and headed for the bathroom.

Paige prepared for the party with particular care, selecting a dress of deep blue-green chiffon that emphasized the long lines of her body. Strappy black sandals, an antique beaded purse, and her mother's pearl earrings were her only accessories, and as she stood before the mirror she was very pleased with her transformation. This afternoon she had watched Grant Hamilton dismiss her as a woman found wanting, and tonight she had curled her hair, taken time with her makeup, and worn her most frivolous dress to deliberately destroy her usually businesslike demeanor. With her auburn hair waving softly down her back, the sensuous movement of chiffon against her flesh, and the subtle hint of Chanel No. 5 wafting around her, Paige felt arresting and very ready for the evening ahead.

Arthur Franklin's home was a rambling, turreted Victorian perched high on the bluffs that overlooked the river. As Paige maneuvered her Toyota into a space on the circular driveway, she reflected how incongruous her car seemed parked beside Mercedes-Benzes and Jaguars. More from force of habit than necessity she locked her car doors before moving up the walk. Once inside, she was impressed, as always, by the well-researched restoration Franklin and his wife had done on the house. The wide entryhall was a showplace for the rich cherry paneling and intricately carved staircase, which were lighted by a chandelier of brass and cut crystal. The hall opened into a double parlor that skillfully blended ornate period pieces with contemporary furniture and art.

As usual, the Franklins had created the perfect mix of guests, too, including museum personnel, area business and social leaders, and professors and their wives from the local universities. The evening was spiced with just the right number of well-known artists, who always seemed willing to fly in at Arthur Franklin's invitation.

In one corner of the room a flamboyant woman ceramicist was holding court, discoursing on the blatantly erotic nature of her latest stoneware creations. In another area designer-clad matrons were putting their carefully-coiffed heads together for a bit of gossip while their husbands stood at the makeshift bar comparing notes on the stock market.

Across the way Paige saw Evan Rogers, the museum's conservator and her mentor, decked out in several splendid examples from his collection of Zuni Indian turquoise. Arthur Franklin stood at the center of his own group—whose members, Paige suspected, would write substantial checks to the museum before the evening was over. As always, the party was well choreographed, put together with equal parts good food, fine liquor, mellow music, and sparkling conversation.

Paige was about to launch herself into the festivities when someone touched her arm. The slight, sensual rasp of a palm sliding along her smooth, bare flesh sent shivers chasing along her spine; she was struck by the warmth and intimacy of the contact. She turned slowly to face the tall man at her side, curious to know why he aroused such a delicious response in her. Then, as recognition swept over her, she stood staring at him, mouth agape.

It was Grant Hamilton.

CHAPTER
Two

"GRANT HAMILTON!" Paige finally managed to exclaim.

The dazzling, sunny grin he turned on her had a devastating and totally unexpected effect. He had not been smiling at the museum this afternoon, and she'd had no way to prepare herself for her rush of response. Involuntarily she smiled back.

"I thought it was you here in the doorway," he was saying in a voice as warm and vital as his smile, "but I could hardly believe my eyes. Do you have a fairy godmother stashed somewhere?"

It took Paige a moment to respond to his offhand compliment. "I don't know what you mean," she lied, pleased he'd noted her appearance.

"This afternoon, you looked"—he grimaced extravagantly—"like someone who played field hockey in college."

Paige laughed. "I did, and I was very good at it, too."

"I don't doubt that. It's just that tonight you look so... so different."

"You're aware that in this day and age judging a woman by her physical packaging is considered gauche, archaic, chauvinistic—"

"I stand rebuked and corrected," he conceded. "And I'll freely admit that I'm as daunted by your competence and ferocious intelligence as by your good looks. Your transformation just took me by surprise."

"I only wear my glasses for close work," Paige felt compelled to explain, "and I tuck my hair up to keep it out of the way."

"Well, as long as you only don that guise for the sake of convenience..."

Paige frowned, struck by the careless condescension he seemed to feel for the world at large.

"Whatever are you doing here?" she countered. "I've never seen you at one of Arthur's parties before."

"Actually, attending affairs like this one isn't my usual style. I generally leave black-tie parties to my brother, Anthony, who enjoys them. But since he's in Europe on business, I've been forced to carry on for the family honor."

Standing beside him, with the spicy tang of his after shave in her nostrils and his warm hand still on her arm, Paige felt a purely physical response to his attractiveness. Unsettled by his nearness and at a loss to explain her confusion, she glanced around trying to think of an excuse to escape him.

"Oh, there's my boss, Evan Rogers," she said. "I really need to have a few words with him while he's free." But before she could make good her escape, Grant Hamilton's warm hand tightened on her wrist, trapping her and sending another jolt of giddy delight racing through her.

"Can't your conversation with Rogers wait? I'm just beginning to enjoy your company." There was an imperious attitude in the question that irritated Paige, and she was suddenly suspicious of his motives. Why had he sought her out tonight? And what made him so determined to spend time with her? Did he hope to somehow gain an advantage over her in the matter of the forgery?

She decided to test her theory. "Actually, Mr. Hamilton, couldn't spending the evening with you be construed as fraternizing with the enemy?"

For an instant he seemed nonplussed by the question. "Are we enemies, Paige?" he finally asked.

"It seemed like it this afternoon when you tried to discredit me and threatened to have me fired."

"I thought we were enemies then, too; only now I'm not so sure."

It was a simple enough statement; but Paige couldn't discern his meaning. Still, something in the tenor of his voice melted her resistance.

"There's a pretty good group playing out on the patio," he coaxed. "Why don't we go out and listen for a while?"

The gentle pressure of his thumb against the pulse that beat erratically at her wrist was too compelling, and she failed to voice her intended words of refusal.

A few minutes later they carried their drinks to a wrought-iron bench at the edge of the flagstone patio behind the house. The band was as good as Grant had claimed, and several couples were shuffling around the makeshift dance floor in time to the music. Glass-globed candles hung from trees throughout the property, giving the gathering dusk a golden glow, and gas lanterns lit the steep landscaped path that led from the garden to the foot of the bluffs and the river.

The metal bench was cold against Paige's bare back, and the breeze that blew up from the water made her shiver. Grant Hamilton either felt or saw her involuntary reaction and slid a protective arm around her, drawing her close. Warmth seemed to radiate from the places where their bodies touched, spreading like ripples across a pond until every cell within her tingled with the effect of his nearness. She sensed the command of his height and carriage, the self-confidence in his easy pose. Sitting side by side in the deepening summer twilight, Paige knew Grant Hamilton was watching her as assiduously as she was trying to avoid looking at him. Swelling anticipation filled the silence that blossomed between them.

"I'd like to dance with you," he said finally, rising above her, certain of her response.

His requests were always imperatives, Paige was beginning to notice, a reflection of his family's wealth and power, no doubt. Nor was she in any position to refuse him, even if she had been able to convince herself she wanted to.

The music was from the big-band era, as mellow and provocative as the muted trumpet that carried the melody. Grant held her with gentle authority so that her cheek rested naturally against his and their thighs brushed suggestively as they moved. The sultry rhythm responsible for the random contact between them made Paige intensely aware of every lean, well-muscled inch of him. His smooth-shaven face was close to her lips, and Paige suddenly longed to reach out and taste his skin. The warm, spicy scent of his cologne filled her mind with images of strength and virility, and she willingly succumbed to the insidious pleasure of being held in his arms. As they danced, her fingers crept along one broad shoulder, then breached the satin collar of his dinner jacket so that she could touch the shaggy dark hair that grew long on his neck, thick, heavy, and surprisingly soft.

"I need a haircut, don't I?" he inquired against her ear.

It was an intimate yet mundane comment, and Paige drew back sharply, ashamed of her heightened awareness in the face of his apparent indifference. This man stirred her in ways she couldn't deny, and being out of control always made her a little angry and a little self-conscious.

Yet she moved close to him again. "Yes, you do need a haircut," she whispered as she brushed one extended finger along the wavy thatch covering the rim of his ear. Her gentle touch was a deliberate provocation as she traced the interior convolutions, determined to garner a response in him to match her own. Slowly he turned warm, curious eyes on her, and she realized he wasn't as indifferent as she'd supposed. For a long moment their gazes held. She noticed he was smiling as he lowered his mouth to hers.

His kiss was sweet and soft, tender and yet so compelling that Paige stretched upward to prolong it, wantonly bringing her breasts and thighs against the full length of him. She felt the convulsive tightening of the arm around her back, but was unprepared for the tremor of response that went through him or the questing tongue that parted her lips. He explored the opening slowly, tracing the contours of her pale pink mouth, pausing at the moist corners before tasting her sweetness more deeply.

The contact between them was suddenly so intimate, so right, so intensely pleasurable that all awareness of their surroundings receded like colors through a fog. Paige felt only Grant's body crushed against hers in a total caress, his hands moving along her back, and his mouth devouring hers. She was dizzily sinking deeper and deeper into a world of their own making, where the only concession to reality was their gentle swaying in time to the music. Time ceased to be as his lips moved against hers in light butterfly kisses that fluttered to her cheek, her ear, and the corners of her eyes. She was helpless in Grant's arms, but no more helpless than he seemed to be in hers. Eventually their bodies stopped swaying, though still they didn't step apart.

"The music's over, Paige," he murmured against her ear, his tone soft, slurred, lazy.

Abruptly, remembering where they were, Paige wrenched away from him, blushing to her hairline. Grant's face was flushed, too, but not with embarrassment; his deep-blue eyes glowed with awakened passion.

Flustered, Paige left the dance floor, though the music was starting again, and walked quickly toward the relative darkness at the foot of the garden. As she reached the path that led to the river, Grant caught up with her.

"Paige?" The timbre of his voice as he spoke her name sent a wave of emotion curling through her. "Paige, what's the matter?"

His hand was warm and soothing on her arm, but she shrugged it off. "How can you ask me what the matter is? Surely you realize we just made a spectacle of ourselves out there on the dance floor. We'll be the main source of gossip over Monday morning's coffee."

"Then perhaps we should have found a more secluded place to get acquainted," Grant observed lightly.

Paige's face flamed. After their run-in this afternoon, she hadn't wanted to become better acquainted with Grant Hamilton; yet she had deliberately teased and enticed him. What had ignited between them had been an unwelcome surprise, but Paige was forced to admit that she, not Grant, had instigated the encounter.

Grant seemed to guess at the conflict she felt, for he drew a long breath and said reasonably, "Look, Paige, why don't I get us something to drink? Then maybe we can just sit and talk for a while."

When he received no reply, he disappeared in the direction of the house, leaving her alone. She sank down onto a low stone bench that overlooked the river far below and buried her face in her hands. How could she have been so forward? she wondered. So blatantly seductive? What had possessed her to respond to him as she had? She hastily dismissed the obvious reasons; she was neither impressed by nor attracted to Grant Hamilton, she insisted stubbornly.

Because her own reactions confused her, she preferred to question Grant's intentions in seeking her out. Why had he approached her tonight if not to somehow compromise her position in the matter of the forgery? This afternoon they had been adversaries, but he had deliberately set out to change all that. How easily she had succumbed to his charms!

Abruptly, Paige rose to her feet. Whether she had made a fool of herself or not, she didn't intend to stay around to compound her folly or learn its consequences. She wasn't about to let Grant Hamilton get the best of her.

Her decision made, she skirted the dance floor and house by a wide margin to avoid a chance meeting with anyone who might prevent her escape. Once she had entered the grove of magnolias at the side of the house, she slackened her pace. It was unlikely that Grant would pursue her when he realized she'd given him the slip. He seemed the kind of man who would have no trouble finding other diversions at a party like this one.

As she moved down the driveway toward her car, Paige rummaged in her evening bag for her keys. Her fingers skimmed over the objects inside—her comb, compact, lipstick, and a few crumpled tissues—but she couldn't find what she was seeking. In exasperation she dumped the contents on the hood of the Toyota, sending them rolling in all directions. Still, no keys. She stared at the scattered objects in mingled panic and disbelief, then peered into the car. The missing keys were dangling from the ignition.

"Damn, damn, damn!" she muttered as she tugged on each door in turn, trying futilely to force one open. "Damn, damn, damn!" she exclaimed more loudly in growing frustration.

"Is something the matter, Paige?" a too-familiar voice asked.

Startled, she whirled to face the man emerging from the shadows, knowing even before her eyes came to rest on the long-boned body and sun-streaked hair, that it was Grant Hamilton.

"I don't make a practice of forcing my attentions on women who aren't interested in me," he went on evenly, "but you seemed upset, and I wanted to be sure you were all right before you went roaring off into the night."

"I doubt I'll be roaring off anywhere," Paige informed him in irritation. "I've locked my keys in the car."

If Grant had laughed, Paige couldn't have been held responsible for her actions, but instead he came up beside her and inspected her situation.

"I suppose we could get a hanger and try to raise the lock or even force a window," he suggested.

She shook her head. This wasn't the first time she had locked her keys in the car, and she knew the best solution.

"I have an extra set at home," she admitted, resigned to asking for his help. "I live at the edge of Conway Park. If you'd be willing to drive me there, I could get them."

Wordlessly, Grant led her to a vintage roadster with a vaulted hood and a tire mounted on the trunk. The green and cream convertible was just the kind of car Cary Grant always drove in the movies, and Paige was enchanted in spite of herself.

"I feel like Grace Kelly or Katharine Hepburn or somebody," she quipped as she slid into the low seat. "The car is beautiful. What kind is it?"

Grant gave a quick laugh. "It's a 1934 MG Midget," he told her, gunning the motor. "You should have seen it when I first got it, though. It was a real mess."

Talk of Grant's painstaking restoration of the car occupied them as they sped along the twisting road that followed the river's course, but as they neared the outskirts of the city, silence descended, heavy and oppressive. Once they had dispensed with the subject of the roadster, there seemed to be no neutral topics of conversation left to them.

As Grant settled the MG into the center lane of the expressway that crossed the city, he broached the one subject that had been on both their minds all evening. "What tests will they use at the museum to determine if 'The Lady of Dordrect' is a forgery?"

Paige drew a deep breath, almost relieved that he had asked about the painting at last.

"Well," she began, "beyond the subjective areas of connoisseurship, in which knowing if a painting is 'right' or 'wrong' is based on an expert's familiarity with an artist's style and composition, tests of a work's physical properties can be used to determine its age and authenticity. We already

Portrait of a Lady 17

used low-angle raking light to study the surface texture, and ultraviolet and infrared light to determine the portrait's condition prior to conservation. Under ultraviolet light, any areas of overpainting fluoresce. Infrared shows what's just under the painted surface. For this particular examination we'll probably use X-rays, too."

"What will the X-rays show?" Grant's tone was casual, but his white-knuckled grip on the steering wheel and the rigid set of his shoulders hinted at his true feelings. For an instant sympathy for him filled Paige. Did the painting's authenticity mean so much to him? And if so, why? Was it because he realized that the world would lose one of the seventeenth century's masterpieces if "The Lady of Dordrect" proved to be a fake? Did he care most about the small fortune he would lose if the museum refused to accept the painting? Or was he apprehensive because she'd uncovered his attempt to defraud the museum?

Paige hardened her heart against him. Perhaps the best explanation for Grant Hamilton's curiosity about the tests and his concern over their outcome was based on a fear of arrest for what he'd attempted to do.

"What will the X-rays show, Paige?" he repeated, breaking into her thoughts.

Smiling to herself, she brushed the hair back from her face before answering. It would serve him right to stew in his own juice for a few days while the tests were completed.

"X-rays show varying densities of paint in a work of art," she explained. "They reveal whether the artist did extensive underpainting, or if he painted over an existing picture. In that case, two images would appear on the X-ray, like a double exposure.

"From what we know of Hals's technique, he worked quickly, creating a surface texture with brushstrokes rather than layers of paint. If the painting is genuine, the X-rays will confirm that."

"Will you run those tests yourself?" Grant gave her a sidelong glance, and Paige shook her head.

"No, the conservator, Evan Rogers, will run them. My participation would compromise both the validity of the tests and my position at the museum."

"And are those the only tests that will be run on the painting?" he asked, a hopeful note in his voice.

"Hardly," Paige answered. "A microtome, a slender needlelike device, will be used to take several minute cross-sections of the paint and backing materials. We'll analyze these cross-sections both chemically and microscopically."

"What will you be looking for?" Grant persisted.

"We know the dates when certain pigments came into use, so their appearance in a piece painted prior to that date would raise questions. For example, it's easy to test for Prussian blue, which came into use in 1704. Should that color be discovered in 'The Lady of Dordrect,' we would have conclusive proof that the work is a forgery."

Grant nodded.

"We can also measure the oxidation of the paint, determine the age of the original canvas if the painting hasn't been relined, and even tell what kind of brushes the artist used. Through spectroscopy and neutron-activity analysis we could further test the pigments. But I doubt those two tests will be necessary, because I can tell you right now, Mr. Hamilton, what the tests will show. They will prove beyond the shadow of a doubt that the painting you sold the museum is a forgery."

A frown drew Grant Hamilton's eyebrows together as he savagely accelerated to pass a slower car. "We'll see about that, Miss Fenton," he said grimly. "We'll see."

As Grant came around to the passenger's side of the car, he glanced up at the meticulously restored town houses lining the east side of the street opposite the grassy central square. Every city had at least one neighborhood like Conway Park, where young professional people interested in urban living had rescued fine old houses from decay. These graceful Victorian row houses, with their mansard roofs and tall, narrow windows, were a perfect example of the melding of nineteenth-century design and twentieth-century determination. As he opened the car door and extended a steadying hand to Paige, he turned from admiring the architecture to admiring the well-built woman carefully extricating herself from the seat of the low-slung roadster. He caught a flash of pale thigh beneath her skirt, a momentary glimpse of full breasts as her neckline gaped away, and then Paige was leading him up the narrow brick walk toward an arched double doorway.

Grant followed slowly, a derisive glint in his eyes. He was at a loss to explain how he had so drastically underestimated Paige Fenton this afternoon; he usually had a discerning eye when it came to women. Certainly Paige couldn't be termed pretty in the usual sense, he conceded, but with her thick russet hair tumbling across her bare shoulders and her strong features animated with excitement, she had made a striking and compelling picture as she stood poised in the doorway of Arthur Franklin's home this evening.

Perhaps if he had met her in more favorable circumstances, he might have been more immediately aware of her. Instead, he had been distracted by the museum's charge that "The Lady of Dordrect" was a forgery.

His hands went suddenly clammy with the memory of those minutes in the conservation office, and he drew a deep breath in an attempt to quell his growing apprehension. He had never expected that the Hals portrait would be exposed as a fake—not with the extensive provenance, letters, and bills of sale to establish it as an old master's work; not after the well-known expert on Northern European painting, Phillip Argenta, had proclaimed the painting genuine just prior to the sale.

Nor could Grant help but wonder what effect the negative publicity this discovery was bound to generate would have on Hamilton Corporation and his own position there. For nearly five years he had fought to carve a place for himself within the complex corporate structure, and it was only in the past eighteen months that he had met with any tangible success.

Now the museum's findings threatened the delicate balance of power within the company. If he was arrested or even openly accused of fraud, everything he'd worked for would be jeopardized, and control of the company would land squarely back in his brother's hands. He would do anything, Grant vowed silently, to prevent Anthony from regaining complete control over Hamilton Corporation.

His were grim, troubled thoughts, and he didn't care to dwell on them. Instead he allowed himself to be diverted by the gentle sway of Paige's hips as she climbed the steps to the front door.

The foyer, with its rich burgundy carpet over gleaming parquet floors and its ornate newel post, was illuminated by a glass-globed chandelier that matched the sconces lighting the stairs. On the second-floor landing Paige paused before the door and lifted the mat to reveal a key. Taking it, she resumed climbing until they reached the head of the stairs.

"Forget your keys often?" Grant inquired as she worked the lock.

"With lamentable frequency," she admitted. "Sometimes I misplace them or lock them in the car, like I did tonight. That's why I keep a key downstairs with Mrs. Cameron. Of course, being absentminded is my only fault."

Grant laughed and followed her inside, pausing to look around as she snapped on lights. The apartment was spare and serene, decorated in cream and gray with accents of peach and mellow green that did not detract from the artwork dominating the walls. The large paintings in understated colors were primarily figural abstracts, the pigment applied translucent and thin. Yet the images had a weight and volume

Portrait of a Lady 21

that belied the pale wash of color and delicacy of line. Although he was no expert, Grant knew good work when he saw it and was impressed.

"Yours?" he inquired after he'd taken a closer look at the paintings.

Paige gave a deprecating shrug. "Anyone in my line of work needs a bit of skill with a brush. I have a studio in the back."

"I want to see it," he insisted, sensing her reluctance. With a second shrug she led the way down the narrow hallway past the kitchen and bathroom to the larger of the two bedrooms. A skylight set into the slope of the roof gave a feeling of space and light even though the sky was dark. Beneath the glass stood an easel with a half-finished still life clamped in place. Along the opposite wall leaned several other works in progress. Grant studied each one carefully, then strolled back to where Paige stood waiting in the doorway.

"These paintings are very good, you know," he said softly. "Do you have a gallery that sells your work? I might be interested in buying one of the figurative pieces for my new house."

A flush of pleasure rose in her cheeks until her face actually glowed. He smiled down at her in genuine enjoyment, feeling warm and pleased with himself. Then, as the sweet, classic perfume she wore filled his senses and mingled with the lingering scents of paint and turpentine, he became suddenly aware of her nearness. With a swell of longing he remembered the feel of her body against his and the taste of her lips. He swayed closer.

For a long moment they seemed suspended, like lonely stars in the emptiness of space; then abruptly Paige retreated. "I won't take one cent of your money, Mr. Hamilton," she declared loudly and vehemently, though her voice was unsteady. "Because while you'd ostensibly be paying for one of my paintings, what you'd really be trying to buy is my cooperation in dealing with your problems at the museum."

It was the second time she'd made that accusation, and anger crackled through Grant as he stood over her. He moved menacingly closer and ran a caressing hand along her arm, his eyes dark and hooded. "Then I suppose seducing you wouldn't help my cause either, would it?"

Her mouth fell open with surprise. She stood stunned by his frank admission.

"Go get your keys," he snapped in irritation. "I've wasted enough of my time for one evening."

Paige fled to do as she was told, and ten minutes later they were whizzing back along the expressway in windwashed silence. By the time they had reached Franklin's property, Grant's anger had cooled, and he was feeling contrite. He had probably scared Paige half out of her wits with his threats and foolish leering. He'd let his temper run away with him again. It was one of his less endearing traits, but he hadn't meant to scare the woman off.

She intrigued him. There was something delightful about someone who could be so organized and competent on the job and then carelessly lock her keys in her car. Something surprisingly inconsistent about someone who could coolly and confidently charge him with fraud, then turn vulnerable and unsure in his arms. Then, too, there was his own purely physical response to her—disconcertingly potent, unquestionably unique, shaking him to the core. Regardless of what happened with "The Lady of Dordrect," he'd decided somewhere between Conway Park and Arthur Franklin's home that he didn't intend to lose track of Paige Fenton.

Grant pulled his roadster into an empty space behind her yellow Toyota, flicked off the ignition, and came around to help her out.

"Thank you very much for your help in getting my extra set of keys, Mr. Hamilton," she began primly when she stood beside him, her fingers trapped securely in his helping

Portrait of a Lady

hand. "Now if you'll excuse me, it's getting late and I'm very—"

"Just a minute, Paige." He made his voice purposefully deep and persuasive. "I want to see you again."

She stared at a point in the middle of his chest, as if afraid to meet his eyes. "I thought I made myself perfectly clear. It won't do you any good to gain my favor. I can't help you with your problems at the museum," she reiterated.

"Yes, you made that perfectly clear." Grant frowned down at her. She was quite willing to think the worst of him, and he had let her. "I want to see you anyway. How about tomorrow?"

"I'm busy tomorrow."

"Sunday?"

"No, I'm busy Sunday, too." It was a lie and Grant knew it.

"Monday then," he persisted. "Dinner, seven-thirty."

"You might not want to see me Monday night," she pointed out.

His eyes narrowed. He was very aware that by Monday night they would know the results of the tests on the painting. "Let me be the judge of that. Besides, one way or the other we'll have something to celebrate."

Paige glanced up at him with a start, the irony of his words not lost on her. "No, I can't."

It was clear that no matter what he suggested, she would continue to refuse him. He changed his tactics. "What time are you busy tomorrow?"

"All day." She was obviously becoming impatient. "Look, Grant," she began, "whatever else you are, you're not dense, so please try to understand. I can't help solve your problem with 'The Lady of Dordrect.' I have no influence, no power. If you deliberately sold the museum a forgery, I hope they prosecute you to the fullest extent of the law! Don't you see you're wasting your time pursuing me? I can't help you, and I wouldn't help a—a smooth-talker like you even if I could.

"I don't want to go out with you," she continued. "Not tomorrow, not the next day, not ever. I'm neither attracted to you nor impressed by your family's money. So just let go of my hand and leave me alone."

He let her finish her tirade but maintained a firm hold on her fingers. "Whatever you're doing tomorrow, may I come along?"

Paige gave a frustrated groan, and Grant knew she was finding his obstinacy infuriating, but he waited quietly, sensing also that she was weakening. For an instant an expression that might have been either speculative or mischievous flickered across her face.

"Oh, all right!" She seemed resigned. "If you insist on horning in on my plans, be at my apartment at eight-thirty sharp. And whatever happens, remember you're the one who insisted on tagging along."

Wearing a broad, victorious smile, Grant escorted her to her car and waited as she unlocked it.

"I'll see you at eight-thirty tomorrow." He grinned and tried to maneuver around the door for a good-night kiss, but Paige was too fast for him. She was securely inside before he could catch her.

"Will you make me breakfast?" he shouted through the glass.

Answering him required that she open the window, and Grant ducked inside and found her lips before Paige realized his ploy. There was a momentary struggle before she gave him her response, but the sweet, open-mouthed surrender was well worth the risk of the gambit. He nibbled gently, tasting the promise of infinite delight in her. As the kiss deepened, he felt a slow, almost imperceptible release as if inhibitions and defenses had begun to ease, uncoil, relax. He found himself enchanted by the artless sincerity of her response. When he finally raised his head, his eyes were clouded and dark.

"Will you fix me breakfast tomorrow?" he repeated in a whisper.

For a moment she nearly acquiesced to his flirtations, then Paige drew a swift, angry breath.

"Absolutely not, you—" The rest of her words were lost in the roar of the Toyota's engine. Grant barely had time to step back out of the way before the car shot forward, its wheels spitting gravel.

CHAPTER
Three

THE DREADED KNOCK came at precisely eight-thirty. Paige took her time answering it, gathering up her hat and keys en route to the door. Grant Hamilton stood outside, dressed casually in a navy-blue open-necked pullover, khaki pants, and deck shoes. In the form-fitting shirt that intensified the color of his eyes, his masculine appeal was overwhelming.

There was something so vital about the lean, broad-shouldered man who stood before her that Paige had to hold tight to the doorknob to keep from being swept up in the wave of pure energy he radiated. Her eyes ran over his sun-streaked hair and ruddy skin, his long-legged stance and steady strength, and she swallowed hard. But even as she fought her awareness of him, she could see she was having an equally powerful effect on him.

She had dressed with particular care this morning, and

she could tell from Grant's open-mouthed astonishment that her attire was producing the desired response. Without a word of greeting she shut the door behind her and led him to the street. She unlocked the Toyota and tossed her hard hat and work gloves in the back with her crowbar and sledge hammer before reaching across to unlock Grant's side. Pulling up the legs of her baggy pinstripped coveralls and pressing one work-booted foot to the accelerator while the other worked the clutch, she turned the ignition key and pulled out into traffic.

Watching her smug profile, Grant finally broke the silence. "You're not going to make this easy for me, are you?"

Paige fought to keep from grinning as she maneuvered the car to avoid several hapless pedestrians. "Why should I make it easy when whatever happens is your own fault for insisting on spending the day with me?"

"I know," he conceded, "but I figured I wouldn't get stuck with anything worse than helping with the laundry or grocery shopping."

"I might have been planning to visit my senile Aunt Millicent," she teased, watching him from the corner of her eye, "or making a trip to the dentist."

He considered those possibilities and shrugged. "I get on pretty well with dotty old women, and I can be very sympathetic when the occasion warrants it. But just what do you have planned for today? Are you moonlighting as a construction worker?"

Paige laughed. Grant was taking the situation rather well, she had to admit. "We're going to help some friends of mine rip down a few walls in the house they're rehabilitating."

"You're kidding! Is that really how you spend your time off, tearing out old plaster?"

"If you want to change your mind, I can turn around at the next corner," she suggested.

"No, no," Grant insisted. "I know how to wield a crowbar, if necessary. How did you get roped into this?"

"I enjoy it," she assured him. They were moving steadily

into an older and less fashionable area of town. "Scott, Laura, and I renovated the house I live in now. Because the state university had used the buildings in Conway Park as classrooms before they moved to their new campus, most of the homes were in pretty good repair. We put in new plumbing and wiring and tore out some of the interior walls to enlarge the living spaces. Cutting the hole in the roof for my skylight was the scariest part, but by then we'd done so much we never thought we could do, we just went ahead."

"That building's a real showplace," Grant commented. "You did a fine job."

"I'm glad you think so," she acknowledged with a smile. "I met the Burdetts when the Conway Park area was just opening up. I didn't have a cent to invest, but I was willing to trade free labor and my services as an art historian in return for a partnership in the property we rehabbed. Because of the architectural research I did, the Burdetts' home and several others were listed in the National Registry of Historic Places. That, in turn, made us eligible for state and federal funds for our restoration. We spent every spare moment for nearly nine months getting the place finished, but it was worth it. Now we're co-owners of a prime piece of property, and while I act as landlord there, Scott and Laura have gone on to other projects. This is their fourth house so far," she announced as they pulled up in front of a dilapidated two-story brick structure. "Are you ready?"

"As ready as I'll ever be," Grant mumbled, getting out of the car.

The houses in this area were older and more run-down than the ones in Conway Park, but in spite of the rubble that littered the vacant lots, the rehabbers were evidently making inroads. Further down the block were several recently restored residences that faced their less elegant neighbors from behind a screen of new wrought-iron fencing. Directly across the street stood new, half-finished row houses built in the style of an earlier day, and the people next door were out painting. A pleasant hum of activity and enthu-

Portrait of a Lady

siasm filled the air, Grant noticed as he sauntered up the buckled sidewalk behind Paige.

"This house is about fifty years older than the one in Conway Park," she explained. "See the difference in the roof line?" She gestured toward the straight, symmetrical slope intersected by the tall chimney built into the wall. "Scott and Laura were lucky to find a house this age in such fine condition."

As they stepped through the scarred, paint-encrusted double doors onto linoleum-covered floors littered with crumbling plaster, Grant wondered at Paige's enthusiasm.

"Hello?" Paige called out. "Is anybody home?"

"Up here," a female voice answered.

Gingerly climbing the rickety staircase, Grant followed Paige to a tiny second-floor bedroom at the front of the house. Scott and Laura Burdett were obviously surprised that their friend had arrived with a strange man in tow, but they acknowledged the introductions cordially. Scott was an amiable red-haired giant who dwarfed his slender sweet-faced wife and looked remarkably natural with a wrecking bar clenched in one meaty fist.

Laura, on the other hand, was a porcelain doll: dark haired, dark eyed, with skin like fresh cream. It seemed to Grant that she should be dressed in satins and velvet, not well-worn denim. She should be safe in a prim Victorian parlor, not working in this rat trap of a house. But he had recently learned that looks could be deceiving, and it wasn't a lesson he was anxious to repeat.

"Since Grant neglected to dress for the occasion," Paige began when the initial pleasantries were over, "I was wondering if he could borrow a pair of Scott's coveralls for the day."

"There's a clean pair hanging in the bathroom downstairs," Laura told him. "Since you and Scott are roughly the same size, they should fit."

"It's not that I neglected to dress appropriately," Grant defended himself. "It's just that Paige never gave me any inkling of the treats she had in store for me today."

"I didn't want to scare you off," she retorted sarcastically.

"The hell you didn't," he replied, his square chin set.

Grant heard Laura give a muffled gasp of surprise at their combative tones, and when Paige turned away, Laura broke the strained silence. "The bathroom's at the foot of the stairs, Mr. Hamilton. Just look for the mauve-flowered curtains in the doorway."

Grant's gaze lingered on Paige before he turned to go. "I'm sure I can't miss it, Mrs. Burdett. Thank you."

Paige was glad that the sharp words she and Grant had exchanged had precluded any curious questions Scott and Laura might have asked about Grant. How could she explain his presence when she didn't understand it herself? Just why had he been so anxious to spend time with her? What did he hope to gain?

Paige snapped her protective goggles and mask in place and reached for her hard hat and crowbar. She didn't want to wonder why Grant had sought her out; she was afraid she wouldn't like the answers.

Ripping down old plaster proved to be a catharsis for Paige, and she attacked the wall with a zeal that sent chips and lattice flying. It felt good to use her muscles and test her strength in work that was satisfyingly destructive yet moved toward a constructive end. Over a hundred years of accumulated dirt and soot came down with the walls until miniature universes of dust motes and plaster particles swirled in the sunlight. Large chunks fell with a rumble that sent turbulent clouds of white eddying upward to hang in the thick, still air.

Thoroughly immersed in her demolition work, Paige was hardly aware when Grant returned, dressed in his borrowed clothes. Later still, she realized he was diligently ferrying Laura's buckets of rubble to the dumpster out back. It was the most demeaning job, and Paige felt perverse pleasure in seeing the high and mighty Grant Hamilton dirtying his carefully manicured hands with manual labor. Yet he worked all morning without complaint, and when Paige called him to come to lunch, it was with a grudging respect for his fortitude. There was an air of satisfaction about him as he slid the last load of debris out the bedroom window down the chute to the trash pile and went outside to eat.

They sat on the front steps together, enjoying the rest, the sunshine, and the food Laura had packed—thick ham sandwiches on homemade bread, slices of sharp cheese, fruit, soft drinks, and beer. As they ate they discussed the morning's progress and the Burdetts' plans for the house.

Through their excited words and detailed descriptions, a vision of the house began to take shape, melding the charm of bygone days with a promise of the future. An ardent preservationist, Paige had always been fascinated by this kind of transformation and appreciative of the hard work that made it possible, but Grant was only beginning to understand. She saw a flare of enthusiasm in his eyes as he began to see the building's potential and share Scott and Laura's dreams. Soon he was making suggestions of his own for landscaping and interior improvements, showing a practical knowledge of construction that surprised her.

Sitting back against the sun-warmed bricks, she eyed Grant analytically, realizing she didn't even know what he did for a living. She frowned and took a swig of beer. People with as much money as the Hamiltons really didn't need to "do" anything, yet the Hamilton Corporation seemed to be a growing concern. He must work there in one capacity or another, she reasoned.

Paige finished off her beer and glanced down the street, trying to convince herself she didn't really care to know any more about Grant. In two day's time, when the results of the tests were in, he would leave her life forever, and the less she knew about him, the less there would be to forget.

All too soon Scott was standing over them, urging them back to work.

"You're a cruel taskmaster," Paige complained as she rose to her feet.

"So I am, so I am," Scott agreed congenially. "By the way, did you bring those proposals for funding I asked you to look over?"

"Oh, Scott, no. I'm sorry. I left them at the museum, though I did have time to read through them. The house is definitely architecturally significant, so I don't think there will be any trouble getting state money for the restoration."

"I want to file them on Monday," Scott prodded her.

"I'll get them from my office tonight and drop them off tomorrow, if that's all right."

"Sure." He nodded as he turned to go inside. "And Grant, before we get back to work, I'll try to find those extra safety goggles, if you still want them."

"No, never mind," Grant assured him. "I really don't need goggles for what I'm doing."

The afternoon grew warm, and the dust and soot combined with their sweat to create a gritty film that coated every inch of exposed skin. The demolition especially had become a hot, unpleasant task, and as Scott began on the last wall to be removed on the second floor, Grant took the wrecking bar from Paige's hands.

"Let me relieve you," he offered. "I can't let you have all the fun."

As tired as she was, Paige conceded willingly and went to stand beside Laura in the doorway. The exercise she'd so welcomed during the morning had finally paled, and her arms and shoulders ached.

The two men worked well together, making short shrift of the central section of the wall. Then as Grant moved to rip out the upper corner, Paige abruptly realized what was about to happen.

"No, Grant! Stop!" she cried out, but before he could react to her warning, a shower of plaster dust and paint flakes was falling into his upraised, unprotected face.

She knew instantly that he couldn't have escaped unscathed, but it was the tense, bent, hands-on-knees pose he assumed and the curse ground out between clenched teeth that alerted her to the seriousness of the accident.

"Is it your eyes, Grant?" Paige asked as she reached him.

He growled an affirmation. "Those damned flakes of plaster feel like boulders, and they're beginning to sting."

As he stood erect, she could see the spray of gray-white dust across his cheeks and the tiny chips caught in his lashes.

"Keep your eyes closed and don't rub them," she instructed calmly, taking his hand. "Now, we're going down to the bathroom. Can you manage the stairs?"

"I'll manage," he mumbled, his expression grim.

As they executed the steep, curving staircase with painstaking care, Paige maintained her calm by dint of will. She could feel the urgency in Grant's grip, and she knew what he must be suffering, but she dared not rush him and chance a misstep. Silently she blessed Laura for insisting on having the first floor plumbing hooked up before the restoration began, so at least there would be water with which to bathe Grant's eyes. While they moved slowly downward, one part of her brain was busy trying to dredge up all the first-aid training she'd ever received. Another was plotting a route to the nearest hospital emergency room.

Laura had run ahead to turn on the taps of the ancient porcelain sink, and as Paige led Grant toward it, she instructed him on how to bathe his eyes to avoid further irritation. He did as he was told with a single-minded diligence that edged on frenzy, and as she watched him, she sensed the rising panic he was holding in check. Gently patting his shoulder in a gesture of reassurance and comfort, she left him splashing in the sink with Scott to watch over him, and dragged Laura into the kitchen.

"Do you have any vinegar here at the house?" she demanded.

"Yes, it's with the cleaning supplies." Laura gave Paige a bottle from a cluster of others on the rickety counter. "Why do you want it?"

Paige washed out a plastic bowl left over from lunch, poured a bit of vinegar into it, then filled the container with water. "There's bound to be lime in that plaster," she explained as she worked. "A mild vinegar solution will neutralize it without hurting Grant's eyes." She took a fresh styrofoam cup from the lunch basket and started toward the bathroom.

"How's it going?" she asked as she reached the sink.

"It's better now, but my eyes still sting like crazy."

"All right, Grant," she instructed, "wash your eyes out once more and then sit on the floor with your back to the tub. There, that's good. Now lean back until your head is resting on the rim." Laura handed her a towel for Grant to use as a pillow. "All right, fine. Next I'm going to rinse your eyes with a solution of vinegar and water. It should take away the stinging." Paige gave the directions with such cool confidence that Grant obeyed without question.

She bent down on her knees beside him so she could look down into his upturned face. As she moved closer, his arm came around her waist, his grip almost painfully tight. With that totally involuntary gesture he revealed a momentary insecurity and a need for reassurance that turned Paige weak and quivery inside. With a soft, light touch she brushed back the wet hair that clung to his temples.

"It's going to be all right, Grant, really it is," she told him quietly, and found that hearing those words spoken aloud calmed her as well.

With a cupful of vinegar solution in one hand, she bent above him and began to bathe one eye, then the other, gently pulling at the corners of his eyelids so the cool soothing water could wash away every particle of plaster. Paige repeated the process over and over, mixing more of the vinegar and water as she needed it.

Pressed intimately against Grant as she worked over him, Paige could accurately gauge his response to the treatment and his level of discomfort. Injuries to the eyes required gentle, patient care, but eventually she felt the tension in his body ebb and the grip on her waist slacken.

"How are you?" she finally asked, sitting back on her heels.

Grant sat up gingerly. "Okay, I think. At least my eyes don't hurt anymore."

"That's wonderful," Laura exclaimed from the doorway where she and Scott had been hovering, ready to help if needed.

"It does seem rather miraculous, considering the shape I was in a little while ago," Grant agreed. There seemed to be more he wanted to say, but the words stayed inside him, and the silence became tentative and prolonged.

"Well, as long as you're sure you're all right, Grant," Scott broke in at last, "I think we'll close things up here so we can all go home. Come on, Laura; help me gather up everyone's stuff."

They left Paige and Grant sitting in the middle of the bathroom floor. As they remained there together, Grant found he was suddenly a little shy and unsure with Paige. She had seen him with his defenses down, and he was no more willing than any man to admit to moments of weakness. Besides, she had taken such competent care of him when he needed it, he was feeling at a distinct disadvantage.

When he spoke at last, he addressed her formally. "I'd like to thank you for what you just did," he began. "Things certainly could have been a lot worse for me if you hadn't known just what to do."

Paige realized what she should say to put Grant at ease, but words failed her as she sat taking in his reddened eyes, his matted hair, and the huge damp spots on his coveralls. Until that moment, she'd had no time to think about how close he'd come to serious injury, about her responsibility in the accident, or about just how frightened she had been, despite her calm exterior. The memory of those first terrible moments when his pain had been so apparent were fresh in her mind, and she couldn't help but wonder if she was worthy of the implicit trust he'd placed in her. Then, suddenly, there were tears on her face, unexpected, inexplicable tears sliding helplessly from beneath lowered lashes.

Giving a muffled exclamation of surprise, Grant pulled her into his lap as reaction and relief overwhelmed her. He held her close as she burrowed against his shoulder, weeping silently. To him it seemed almost inconceivable that the Paige Fenton he knew could be huddled in his arms seeking comfort. Yet her curious vulnerability wasn't completely foreign to him. Murmuring comforting words against her hair, he drew her closer still, enjoying the sensation of strong, competent Paige nestling against him. Grant smiled contentedly. To be able to fulfill her needs, as she had so amply seen to his, left the warmth of satisfaction deep within him.

Fresh from a steamy shower and clad only in a towel, Paige faced her gaping cupboards, wondering what to serve her unexpected dinner guest. Just how Grant had managed to wangle an invitation, Paige wasn't sure. Doubtless he had played on her sympathies, and since she felt responsible for his accident this afternoon, she had been unable to refuse him. Even though the doctor in the emergency room she'd insisted they visit had praised the first aid Grant had received, Paige knew she was negligent in not insisting he wear safety goggles, and foolhardy in letting him tag along in the first place. Now, for all her sins, she was stuck with feeding him a meal and putting up with his company this evening.

Undoubtedly she'd get through it somehow, but at the moment her problem was deciding what to serve. Like Old Mother Hubbard's, her cupboard was very nearly bare, and she had no hope of replenishing it before Tuesday when her paycheck would come. Museums all seemed to assume that their employees worked for the love of art, not to put bread on the table. Those on the staff not blessed with a trust fund or stocks lived from payday to payday, as Paige did. From the meager stores on hand, the best she could concoct was a supper of tuna casserole and salad. It would be an inelegant meal, but it served Grant right for forcing himself on her. She put salted water on the stove to boil while she went to dress.

She selected her clothes with the same meticulous care she had taken the night before, but now for the opposite effect. At Franklin's party she had tried to appear frivolous, soft, and alluring, but tonight she was returning to her businesslike self: to the woman Grant had so obviously found wanting. It was a test of sorts, but Paige wasn't sure what she hoped to prove.

The problem was she couldn't convince herself that Grant's interest in her was genuine, without ulterior motives. Why else would a handsome, personable man waste his time pursuing a woman like her? Oh, her hair was a nice color and her teeth were straight, she was willing to admit, but essentially she was plain. And yet, last night he had found it expedient to be charming, persuasive, seductive.

What he clearly wanted in playing this attentive role was her help in dealing with his dilemma at the museum. Hadn't he admitted as much? Why was she so reluctant to believe the worst of him? Attractive, virile men like her father, like her long-lamented only love, Patrick Marshall, and like Grant Hamilton used women to their own ends and then discarded them. It was a lesson she had learned early in life and seemed destined to learn again and again. She might as well admit Grant was drawn to her only because of some advantage he hoped to gain in the question of the Hals portrait. She would be wise to remember that, she observed, and maintain a distance.

Stepping in front of the mirror, she buttoned the simple chocolate-brown blouse she had selected and tucked it into ivory linen slacks. With her heavy hair twisted into a knot at her nape, gold hoop earrings and her watch as her only accessories, and low-heeled sandals on her feet, she looked cool, tailored, and supremely businesslike. With a satisfied smile on her lips she went resolutely toward the kitchen.

She set the table with everyday china and paper napkins, put on candles and then removed them, put them back and removed them a second time. She wasn't trying to impress Grant Hamilton, she reasoned with unusual truculence. If the meal proved less grand than what he was used to, what did it matter?

Grant arrived with a bottle of wine under one arm and both hands full of wildflowers. Thinking he did indeed mean to buy her cooperation in the matter of the forgery, Paige had expected long-stemmed roses at the very least, and the bunches of wildflowers both pleased and confused her.

They ate a silent meal, letting the jazz and classical music on the stereo fill the gaps in the conversation. Paige refused to apologize for the simple fare, and if Grant found her culinary talents lacking, he was polite enough not to mention it. Once the dishes were washed and put away, the evening stretched before them like an endurance course, the minutes looming like obstacles to be hurdled. Paige cast around frantically for something to keep them safely occupied until she could plead fatigue and send Grant packing. She smiled with sudden inspiration.

"I need to stop by the museum this evening to pick up the proposals I promised Scott. You don't mind, do you?" It was a request he could not refuse. Yet it was clear he had other things in mind.

"It's after hours at the museum, isn't it?" he asked pointedly, but Paige was already taking a small address book from a drawer in the kitchen and punching the numbers for the security office.

"That's all right, Grant. I work late a lot," she confided as the number rang. "Hello, Alan? It's Paige Fenton... Fine. And you?... Look I left some papers in my office I need first thing tomorrow, and I'd like to stop by and pick them up... Yes, I know the policy... Well, this won't be the first time... Yes, I know... I know... Please, Alan. I really do need them... Right. At the service entrance in twenty minutes. Thanks, Alan, you're a lifesaver."

With a gleam of triumph in her eyes, she turned to the tall man lounging in her Barcelona chair. "Come on, Grant. We're in."

As Grant drove through the muffling twilight, street lamps and porch lights began to come on, giving the city streets a warm, intimate glow. Paige heard parents calling their children home to bed, the forlorn jingle of an ice-cream truck making its last stops, the country music that drifted from the jukebox in the corner bar. The wind began to stir the elms and maples overhead, bringing the cool, loamy smell of approaching night.

Ignoring the irritated expression on Grant's face, Paige stole a look at her watch. It was just after eight-thirty. If she was careful, she could stretch this errand to take the better part of an hour, and by nine-thirty surely she could feign fatigue and ask to be taken home. It had been an exhausting day, after all. Then there would only be the meeting on Monday to be endured, when the tests on "The Lady of Dordrect" would be made public. After that, if she was right about Grant's motives, he would walk out of her life forever. And when he did, her biggest satisfaction would be knowing that she had not succumbed to his charms.

As they topped the rise where the museum stood, Paige felt the usual tingle of response as the massive structure came into view. Built shortly before the turn of the century, the main building was of unyielding gray stone in a style known as Richardsonian Romanesque. Of massive proportions, the facade looked like a castle with turrents at each end and had rounded archways across the entrance. Clearly it was a building designed to safeguard treasures and withstand the ages.

The service entrance was located in the new wing at the back. Alan Fellows opened the door at Paige's knock and frowned deeply when he saw the man at her side.

"I assumed you would be alone, Paige," Alan chided

her. He had joined the museum staff as assistant security supervisor a year before, and during Paige's frequent late-night stints in the conservation lab, a comfortable friendship had grown up between them. Though he bent the rules occasionally in her behalf, he maintained a deep sense of responsibility toward the artwork entrusted to his care.

"Alan Fellows, may I present Grant Hamilton." She saw the black man's brows lever upward with recognition of the Hamilton name. If he had been about to deny Grant entry, he abruptly changed his mind.

"You go on and get what you need from your office, Paige. I've turned off the interior sensors between here and there, but stop at 'Big Brother' on the way back so I can let you out. And be careful. Hal Anderson is at the other end of the building on his rounds. Mind you, don't scare each other to death in one of those dark galleries."

"Big Brother" was the name the museum staff had given the complex computerized security system installed several years previously, Paige explained to Grant as they crossed the vaulted main hall of the museum. With nothing more than the glare of the occasional EXIT signs to guide them, they made their way through the warren of adjoining rooms and galleries to the third floor, which housed the administrative offices, workshops, and conservation labs. Since the sensor light on her door shone green in the darkened hallway, she turned her key in the lock, snapped on the overhead lights, and headed for her glass-enclosed cubicle at the far end of the room. She rummaged noisily through her desk, pretending to search for the documents Scott had given her. When she felt she had wasted enough time, she took the papers out of the top drawer where they had been all the time and turned to go.

Across the room Grant Hamilton was standing over the Hals portrait, his expression dark and troubled, and she couldn't help but wonder what he was thinking. For an instant she felt an urge to comfort and reassure him as she had in different circumstances this afternoon. But she could not. On Monday the tests on "The Lady of Dordrect" would be finished, and he would have to face the consequences of selling the forgery. But then, she no longer felt sufficiently vindictive to taunt him with her certain knowledge of the findings. Instead she came up beside him and gently took his hand.

"Come on, Grant. Let's go," was all she said.

They made a leisurely circuit of the city, beginning with the prestigious area of old homes near the museum known as "the bluffs," to the noisy, glitzy riverfront, then back through rows of stores closed for the night and sleepy residential streets to Conway Park.

"Well, Paige," Grant said when he had parked the car, "shall we go somewhere and get a drink, or are you going to invite me in?"

His blunt question surprised her, and it took a minute for her to voice the little speech she had been rehearsing since they'd left the museum. "I'm sorry, Grant. It's been a trying day, and I'm tired." Even in her own ears the words sounded trite and hollow, yet she raised her head defiantly, determined to escape him.

His heavy dark brows drew together in a frown as he studied her face in the lamplight.

"You know, you're a coward, Paige," he accused softly. "Afraid of everything you can't control, everything that isn't museum perfect. I realized tonight how well that place suits you. There you're safe in your ivory tower, protected from the rest of us by your icy detachment and your pretentious intellectualism. And you keep your own treasures as carefully guarded as exhibits under glass. Your warmth, your tenderness, your vulnerability are untouched, as inviolate as the objects in that damned museum."

His voice was low, harsh, tinged with anger, and Paige sat staring, trying to comprehend his reactions. Then the hand that had rested innocently along the back of the seat was pulling the pins from her hair, sending an auburn torrent tumbling down her back. His fingers tangled in the loosened strands, holding her fast when she would have pulled away as his other arm came possessively around her. For an instant she struggled against him, painfully aware of the emergency brake prodding her and the gearshift tangled with her legs. Then Grant moved slightly, and there was only the weight of his body along hers and the intoxicating power of his kisses.

Panic licked along her nerves, only to be dispelled by waves of slowly encroaching pleasure. She tried to turn her head away, but the play of his mouth against hers was subtle and insidious, fueling the fire suddenly blazing within her.

As before, Paige was unprepared for her reactions to Grant, for the utter dissolution of will he seemed to engender in her. Was her response to him the result of something unique that passed between them, or was Grant's touch so potent and delightful because it had been such a long and lonely time since any man had held her as he did? Surely Patrick had made her feel like this once, hadn't he? It was so desperately hard to remember.

Grant's mouth poised over hers, and she could see it was twisted derisively. "Stop thinking, damn you! This isn't something to be analyzed and catalogued." Then he was kissing her again, fiercely, ferociously, demanding her response. But even as his lips plundered hers, his hands were gentle, cherishing. The contradictions so obvious in him filled her with incoherent wonder, and then her own thoughts went wispy and floated away, like morning fog beneath an insistent sun.

She came to him willingly at last, her arms encircling his neck as she returned his kiss, her body arching against him. Their pleasures seemed to expand out of proportion to the simple intimacies they allowed themselves, yet neither Paige nor Grant questioned the magic flowing between them. In the cool summer evening they sat kissing and embracing for a very long time, lost in the delight each found with the other. But when Grant eventually suggested that they go inside, a swift alarm raced through Paige, dispelling the languoruos aura of passion that had engulfed her and replacing it with sudden sobriety.

"No! Oh, no!" Paige retreated from him as far as the confines of the small foreign sportscar would allow. "I intended to go in by myself long ago, and none of this has changed my plans."

Grant, plainly frustrated, glowered at her across the width of the car. "Why are you determined to make this difficult, Paige? We're two mature adults who are attracted to each other. Why can't you just let nature take its course?"

"Oh, no, Grant. I'm one mature adult attracted to another, but it's clear you're plotting seduction with the hope of gain."

"You don't seriously believe that, do you?" he demanded.

"Last night you admitted that seducing me was part of your plan to win an advantage in your conflict with the museum. Why deny it?"

Grant glanced away, his mouth drawn and his chin set. "I was angry last night. I didn't mean what I said."

"You're angry now," she fired back. "How can I believe what you're saying tonight?"

He recoiled as if her words had stung, and sat staring at her for a long moment. Then he was across the car in one predatory leap, pinning her against the door, his grip on her shoulders unrelenting.

"You're right, I am angry now, but I promise you, you can believe everything I say." He was so close she could feel the wash of his warm breath across her cheeks as he spoke and see the blaze of blue fire in his eyes. "What I want from you, Paige Fenton, has absolutely nothing to do with that damned painting!" His words were slow, clipped, and clear, and the pressure of his fingers was beginning to hurt. Paige had never imagined Grant could be so threatening, so ruthless, so close to losing control. Abruptly his hands dropped from her arms, but he held her immobile with the intensity of his gaze. "You do believe what I'm saying now, don't you, Paige?"

She swallowed hard and nodded, frightened of this new side of Grant Hamilton. In the momentary lull that followed her answer, she sprang from the car and fled up the walk to the safety of her apartment.

CHAPTER
Four

BACON.

The sweet smell of cooking meat assailed Paige even in the depths of sleep: pungent, mouth-watering, unmistakable.

Bacon?

Who on earth was cooking bacon? Her mind was beginning to stir in spite of her. Tentatively she opened one heavy-lidded eye and saw daylight seeping around the edges of the pleated paper window shade. It must be morning, she conceded, and burrowed deeper into her pillow. Sleeping late on Sunday was one of the luxuries she had always allowed herself. Still, the smell of sizzling bacon persisted and was soon joined by the aroma of perking coffee. They were breakfast smells that must be wafting up from Mrs. Cameron's apartment.

Abruptly the slam of a cupboard door in the next room

brought her upright in bed, startled and disbelieving. Now that she was fully alert, she could hear the pop and crackle of frying meat and the scrape of a fork on the side of a metal bowl. Someone was in her kitchen, she realized suddenly, then tore back the covers and padded barefoot down the hall, more curious than frightened. Dangerous intruders generally didn't stop by to cook breakfast.

In the kitchen Grant Hamilton stood in the midst of culinary disorder with fork in hand. Egg shells were scattered across the counter while a frosty pitcher of orange juice frothed beside the sink. There was a mound of grated cheese on the cutting board and a half-filled platter of bacon next to the stove. Wearing a sunny oxford-cloth shirt and a towel tucked into the waistband of his crisp jeans as a makeshift apron, Grant looked oddly at ease in Paige's kitchen.

"Oh, good morning, Paige," he greeted her as he put bread in the toaster. "Finally awake, I see."

"I could hardly help it with the racket going on in here. What the hell are you doing in my kitchen?" she demanded.

Grant ignored her gruffness and favored her with one of his melting smiles. "Why, I came to serve you breakfast in bed," he explained sweetly. "In payment and apology for last night."

He did owe her an apology for his behavior when he'd brought her home, but Paige was suspicious of his motives in showing up this morning. Undoubtedly he was hoping to enjoy far more than breakfast in her bed.

"And I suppose you expect me to share it with you," she accused, color mounting to her cheeks.

"Don't you think it would be a little selfish to deny me that when I've gone to all this trouble?" he admonished her.

She came a step nearer as angry words bubbled to her lips; she was furious that he could be so presumptuous. "I don't know what gave you the idea I'd sleep with a man because he cooked me breakfast," she railed, "but you're dead wrong. I think far too much of myself to sell my favors so cheaply. How you dare—"

Portrait of a Lady 47

Grant's whoop of delighted laughter cut her short, and although she wasn't quite sure what she'd said, she knew his amusement was at her expense. "I was talking about sharing breakfast, Paige," he explained between chuckles. "Just what was it *you* were planning to share?"

A flush of mortification colored her cheeks, and she fervently wished she'd never set eyes on this person who had plundered her kitchen and clearly had designs on her person, even though he denied it. Then she realized she had been standing talking to Grant in nothing more substantial than her nightgown. It was a modest enough garment, high-necked and long-sleeved. But where the sheer batiste skimmed close to her body at her breasts and hips, it revealed far more than she might have wished. Beneath the translucent fabric her skin glowed pale, luminescent pink and tantalized the observer with a promise of the supple contours of her body. From the slow, lazy grin creeping across Grant's features, Paige could guess the trend of his thoughts and fought to suppress her warm shudder of response.

"How . . . how did you get into my apartment?" she inquired unsteadily, determined to focus his attention on something besides the state of her undress.

His eyes never wavered from the button of the nightgown that strained ever so slightly over her full breasts and the erect nipples that tinted the thin fabric a deeper shade of rose. "I knew you kept a key under the mat downstairs. I just borrowed it for a few minutes while I brought up the groceries. You really should find a better place to hide that key, you know. It's not safe."

Paige shrugged at his concern and ran her fingers through her tumbled hair. The unconscious gesture caused the button to gape wide and for a moment afforded Grant a glimpse of her softly rounded, ivory-smooth breasts. "Oh, it's safe enough as long as no one knows that key is for this apartment," she assured him.

The unexpected view of Paige's curves derailed Grant's train of thought and sent hot blood coursing to his loins.

For a split second before he regained control of himself, he considered wrestling this infuriatingly enticing woman to the kitchen floor and making mad, passionate love to her while the bacon burned to cinders. Instead he took a deep breath and moistened his lips.

"Why don't you—um—go back to bed, Paige," he suggested, "and I'll be in as soon as the food's ready." His voice had a slurred, persuasive quality that turned her will to water, but Paige knew this was too provocative a situation to prolong. After yesterday and last night she wasn't sure just how much she could refuse Grant, and she didn't want to put her resolves to the test where he was concerned.

"No. Oh, no. The prospect of your presence in my bedroom makes me very nervous, so why don't you just set the table out here while I go get dressed. Besides it's...it's slothful to go back to bed once you're up." She made the last statement with a solemnity of tone usually reserved for reciting the Ten Commandments, then marched out of the room.

"Slothful?" she heard Grant mutter as she closed the bathroom door.

There wasn't time for more than the basics, and a few minutes later Paige joined Grant at the table dressed in vintage jeans and a T-shirt with Picasso's signature emblazoned across the front. The food he had fixed was surprisingly good, she conceded as she munched a strip of crispy bacon; but then, anyone could make a decent breakfast.

"All right, now what?" Paige addressed him over the rim of her coffee cup when they were finished. "You didn't come here to cook me breakfast without having some idea of how we'd spend the rest of the day."

Grant sat back in his chair, gauging her expression. "I've given it a great deal of thought, as a matter of fact, but if you have something else you want to do, I'll understand."

It was a chance to demur, to make up some story about going boating with friends or having a tennis date with some fictitious man, and Paige knew it. The fact that Grant had given her an out, if she chose to take it, was as enticing in its way as his mysterious plans. Nor could she help but wonder if he had come to understand her well enough in their short acquaintance to realize she invariably balked when she was bullied. She watched him closely, then shrugged. Maybe he was just being nice.

She set her cup down on the table. "My time's my own today," she told him. "At least, it is after I drop off Scott's proposals. What did you have in mind?"

A gleam of triumph shone in Grant's deep-blue eyes, and she realized he was far more astute than she had supposed.

"Hamilton Corporation is building a subsidiary plant about sixty miles north of here. On my trips back and forth to the construction site I've noticed a number of antique shops and barns along the roadside. I've never had time to stop, but they do look intriguing. And since you seem to enjoy that sort of thing, I thought they might be fun to explore."

Paige was unduly pleased that Grant had tried to take her interests into account when making his plans. "Oh, that does sound like fun," she agreed enthusiastically.

"There's also a man up in Farleyville who specializes in American paintings and folk art," Grant went on. "I've been looking at limner portraits for quite a while, and I'd appreciate your opinion of his collection."

"So it's my professional advice you're really after and not my charming self," she said, pouting.

Grant leaned toward her across the table and covered her hand with his. "If I told you it was your charming self I was really after, would you believe me?"

His abrupt change of manner alarmed and confused Paige, and she snatched her cool fingers from beneath his warm ones. "No, probably not," she admitted uncomfortably. "Actually, it surprises me to hear about your interest in American primitives. I didn't think you were an art collector."

Grant shrugged. "I'm not. Too much in the art world is determined by a painting's worth and not by the work itself.

I buy strictly what I like, but I do try to make wise selections. Besides, it's pretty hard to be without some interest in art when you grow up in a house where everyone poured over sale catalogues from Southeby's the way some families do the ones from Sears, Roebuck."

Grant came to his feet and began to gather up the dirty dishes. "Why don't you get ready to go while I clean up the kitchen," he offered. "And, Paige, thanks for agreeing to come with me."

The hot water beat against Paige's upturned face, rolled along her nose and cheekbones, and dribbled off her chin. It exploded into a fine spray on contact with her chest and shoulders, then sluiced downward over her breasts, belly, hips, and legs to pool around her feet. For a long time she was content to stand perfectly still, letting the soothing warmth and insistent rhythm of the shower work its magic. Outside the confines of this private world Grant Hamilton and confusion awaited her, but here she was safe.

Things had been so easy that first afternoon; she had known just where she stood. Grant had been attempting to defraud the museum, and she had caught him at it. Then it had been so clear; they were adversaries. But now that line had begun to blur. At Arthur Franklin's party Grant had been charming and seductive, and she had temporarily succumbed to his masculine appeal. Still, she had been able to dismiss him as a manipulative opportunist and remain aloof. But yesterday that stereotype had shattered, and she had seen him as an individual: warm, likable, compelling. She'd seen him as a man with humor, enthusiasms, and fears of his own. He had suddenly been lost and vulnerable, wanting and needing her comfort, just as she had later needed his. Was it possible that he really wanted no more of her than what he claimed? Could it be that his interest in her had nothing to do with the forgery?

But it always did come back to that: the forgery. What kind of man tried to pawn off a worthless imitation as a genuine work of art? In spite of Grant's protests Paige knew the portrait was a fake. She had staked her professional reputation on it, and tomorrow she would be vindicated. Was it possible he didn't know the true value of the piece, or had he deliberately tried to cheat the museum? Paige desperately wanted to believe him innocent of any deception, but she didn't know if he was. She knew only she was courting personal disaster by spending time with him. The potent alchemy that existed whenever they were together had the power to decimate her will, and she realized that when he inevitably attempted to make love to her, she would be helpless to refuse him.

The shower's pounding water offered only temporary escape, and she turned off the taps with a murmur of resignation before she began to towel herself dry. A few minutes later she emerged from the bathroom wrapped in her full-length terry-cloth robe and started down the hall toward the bedroom.

"You must be as wrinkled as a prune after all that time in the shower," Grant quipped as she passed the kitchen doorway. But at the sight of her he swallowed whatever else he had intended to say. Her ivory skin was flushed and dewy from the hot water, and he knew that beneath her belted robe she was just as flushed and dewy all over.

He set aside the pan he had been drying and came toward her. If there was a coherent thought in his head beyond his need to touch her, Grant could not name it. Paige shrank away as he came nearer, and he wanted desperately to soothe and reassure her, but there were no words to express what he was feeling.

Instead she read it all in his trembling hands and the uneven rise and fall of his breathing. Though she knew she sealed her doom with the act, Paige slid her arms around his neck and pressed her body full against him. The contact sent aftershocks shuddering through them both, and for an instant they could do no more than cling together. Then his lips captured hers in a kiss that was both a sweet relief and a sizzling provocation. Their tongues played as Grant untwined her towel turban and tangled his fingers in the damp russet masses of her tumbled hair.

Her head fell back as she arched against him, and he traced a tingling path from her pliant mouth to the point of her chin, then along her curving throat to the vulnerable hollow at its base. He continued downward to the shadowed valley between her breasts, noting the rosy flush beneath her skin that budded under the pressure of his lips. As his kisses ascended to the crest of one softly rounded breast and then the other, Grant slid a hand between the folds of her robe and along the firmness of her inner thigh to the very center of her moist warmth. Sparks burst behind her closed eyelids as he stroked deeper and deeper, finding the secret reservoir of her desire, turning her nearly mindless with exquisite pleasure. Her body's convolutions were a subtle unfurling mystery to him, fresh with wanting. And hers was a need that Grant ached to fulfill.

The gentle tug of Paige's teeth against his earlobe and her warm breath in his ear sent shivers washing through him. But it was the insistent hand that stroked rhythmically below his belt that threatened his self-control. He wanted to strip off his clothes and feel her fingers moving over his bare flesh, turning him liquid with desire. He wanted to search for the ultimate delight in her. With furious impatience he pulled her down the hall toward the bedroom, where the consummation of their need could take place in comfort. But Paige hung back.

"Oh, Paige, please," Grant murmured in a husky voice. "I want you so."

Even caught up in the snare of her own raging desires, Paige believed that what she was about to do was wrong; not wrong in a moral sense, but because once she had shared her love with Grant, she could never escape him unscathed. And though she no longer cared about the personal consequences of opening herself to him, she could not risk carrying a child as a result of this encounter, since the affair would inevitably end.

"I want you, too, Grant." She soothed him with a dizzying kiss. "It's just that I need a moment to prepare."

Her meaning brought a certain rationality to his eyes. "I'll take care of that if you'd rather," he offered solemnly.

"No, it's all right. Go into the bedroom; I'll join you in a minute."

He lowered his mouth to hers once more before turning to go, as if to seal his claim on her. But in the end it was as much Grant as Paige who was marked by the promise of ecstacy.

When she came into the bedroom a short time later, Grant was waiting on the far side of the double bed. His clothes had been carefully placed over the director's chair at its foot, and he sat covered to the waist with her candy-striped sheets, his wide shoulders braced against the semicircular rattan headboard. He was more heavily muscled than he had looked through his clothes and was of truly classical proportions.

As she stood just inside the doorway, Paige could not bring herself to meet his eyes or think what to do next. The prospect of slipping off her robe and standing naked before him was simply impossible. But he seemed to understand her reluctance. Without a word he extended one hand to her in a gesture of invitation as old as time.

Paige came to him tentatively, with halting steps that brought her to the bed, with irresolution that left her sitting at the very edge of the mattress as if poised for flight. Grant waited as she settled more comfortably beside him, then gingerly took her hands.

"Why are you so afraid of me, Paige?" he wanted to know.

She hesitated, still unable to look at him. How could she accuse him of duplicity now when she was about to trust him with all she had to give? What words could explain that, in spite of her suspicions and mistrust, she had fallen in love with him? It was impossible to lie to him and then share the ultimate intimacy.

Slowly she looked up into his face. "I'm not afraid of you, Grant. I'm afraid of myself." It was the truth, stated as baldly and as forthrightly as she could speak it, but she gave him no time to contemplate her words. As soon as they left her lips, she moved closer, intending to deliberately render his powers of reason useless. Hovering over him on hands and knees, she kissed him deeply and felt him respond. Her fingers moved over his warm flesh, seeking his nipples in the mat of hair that covered his chest. As they came erect beneath her teasing touch, a moan of pure surrender shuddered through him, and Paige knew he could no more question the meaning of what she'd confessed in that moment of weakness than she could explain.

If she had imagined she could somehow remain untouched by the passion that consumed him, the next minutes proved her wrong. Somehow she found herself lying beneath Grant, her pale-yellow robe drawn open to reveal the whole of her body to him. But her nakedness didn't matter now. She wanted his eyes to feast upon her flesh, wanted his hands to have access to all of her. And Grant took what she offered so freely, finding with his tongue and touch all the secret places that pleased her most. Her breathless gasps of mounting pleasure gave inarticulate proof of her need, and Grant realized she wanted this joining as much as he.

Moving above her, he thrust down to fill her, and for a flash of eternity they lay without moving, each of their senses totally occupied by the other. The moment hung suspended, crystalline, seminal, pure, burning its way into both their memories so it could never fade with time or separation.

"Oh, Paige...Oh, Paige..." Grant murmured at last, half-delirious with the satisfaction of being one with her, half-mad with wanting more and more.

His words shattered the intangible spell that held them,

and they twisted together, seeking a deeper and more profound union. Heat moved through them like a raging fire before the wind: melding them, shaping them, forging them into a more perfect whole. Then ecstacy burst upon them, consuming them in the ultimate consciousness. It flared through their brains and bodies, leaping each synapse, searing each neuron with such intensity that when it was over, they lay spent and dazed by the wonder that had passed between them.

How long they drifted in the hazy aftermath of passion Paige did not know. For a time she was aware of nothing more than the reassuring thud of Grant's heart beneath her ear as she lay sprawled against him, and the gentle hand that smoothed her damp, tumbled hair. It was longer still before she raised her head to look into his deep-blue eyes. Where before they had mirrored his desire and need, they now registered utter calm and undeniable tenderness. With one index finger she traced the contours of his lips, noting their fullness and an innate sensitivity that hinted at a side to his character she had not suspected. For an instant she nearly succumbed to the very real temptation of kissing him again and chancing whatever it might bring, but Grant nipped playfully at her finger, and she retreated, smiling.

"You don't have any idea how truly lovely you are, do you?" he said as he watched her. "With that glorious hair and petal-smooth skin. And I bet no one has ever told you that your eyes are the exact color of polished jade."

After his careless contempt of two days before, the words brought sweet satisfaction, but now everything between them was miraculously changed. Only the situation at the museum was the same.

Paige shrugged the discordant thought away and smiled at him from beneath her lashes. "You mustn't tease me, Grant," she demurred.

"Don't you think I know the color of polished jade?" he challenged good-naturedly. "Well, I do. My mother wore a ring just the shade of your eyes. It had a round jade stone set with pearls on either side, fashioned after the one 'The Lady of Dordrect' is wearing. Have you noticed it in the painting?"

Paige shook her head.

"My father had it made for her just after they were married because my mother loved that portrait so. There were times as I was growing up when I fancied 'The Lady' meant more to her than Anthony and I did."

Grant's eyes were dark and clouded as he spoke, and when he paused for breath, Paige sensed he had not meant to talk so freely. Yet he seemed compelled to continue.

"The ring never left her finger until the night she died. She had a stroke as she was preparing for bed and was dead before she reached the hospital. Afterward we found the ring on father's nightstand, as if she'd known what was about to happen and had left it there to comfort him.

"Oh, Grant, I'm sorry," she whispered.

"Father carried the ring with him everywhere until he died. I suppose Anthony has it now since he and Mother were always close."

Beneath the explanation lay a morass of unspoken emotions, of unresolved conflicts, the nature and extent of which Paige could only guess. She curved closer, intending the intimacy to be a balm for his obvious pain and uncertainty.

"If 'The Lady of Dordrect' is so important to your family, why did you agree to sell it to the museum?" The question came from her deep concern for Grant and an earnest need to understand his motives, so she was unprepared for the stiffening of his body beside her and the rigidity of the arm he'd draped casually across her shoulder. Surprised, she turned to look up into his set face and was shaken by the expression in his artic-blue eyes.

"That's none of your damned business, Paige, and I don't intend to discuss my actions with you!" he told her gruffly as he came to his feet on the far side of the bed. "The decision to sell 'The Lady of Dordrect' was mine—mine alone—and I accept full responsibility for it, as well as its consequences. And if you want to spend the rest of the day with me, you'd better get up and get dressed." Without another word he gathered up his clothes and strode toward the bathroom.

Paige stared after him in astonishment, unable to fathom what had upset him.

CHAPTER
Five

THE COUNTRYSIDE WAS spectacular with summer's golden sunshine brushing rust-tinged leaves to cast dappled shadows across the roadway, with fields being swiftly shorn of ripening grain, with fruit stands riotous with a bounty of delicious color. Lazy clouds sprawled across a meadow of azure sky as a gentle but insistent breeze shepherded them toward a distant horizon. Birds wheeled in graceful patterns high above or effortlessly rode invisible currents in the air, while the quicksilver flash of a jet sketched contrails in the atmosphere. Even the highway, with its undulations and sweeping curves creeping across the broad Midwestern hummocks, added to the easy flow of the day.

Yet as Grant piloted the roadster along the gentle dips and turns, he was aware of the uncomfortable silence in the car. What should have been a companionable outing with a woman he liked and admired had subtly changed into something less than what he had envisioned. Making love should have bonded them together, but he knew he himself had forced them apart.

Though his attention was on the road stretching before him, he was intensely aware of the woman at his side. He saw the flush of sunlight on her creamy skin and the way it caught in the heavy braid that hung across one shoulder, turning the lustrous auburn hair a deep, rich red. The trim plaid blouse and olive-green pantskirt that skimmed the now familiar contours of her body offered a subtle invitation that more provocative garments might not. To know the beauty and sensuality that lay just beneath the tailored trappings teased his imagination. He longed to strip away the clothes to expose her once more to his ravenous desires.

It had been a long time since any woman had so intrigued him after the first blaze of lust was extinguished. But in spite of the satisfaction he'd found in this morning's joining, a smoldering ember of need still glowed within him. The possibility of making love to her again and again in various ways and circumstances piqued his curiosity. And instinctively he knew no matter how often he drank the cup of passion to the dregs, with Paige it would always be miraculously refilled.

For an instant he turned his eyes from the road to glance at her beside him. The sunglasses high on the bridge of her nose effectively masked her expression, but the hands lying tensed in her lap suggested that she was as uneasy as he. Regret washed over him at the knowledge that his own inability to trust her with his secrets had spoiled the intimacy they had shared.

For the dozenth time in these past days he wished he could explain to her about the painting. But he knew he could not. The decision to offer 'The Lady' to the museum, and whatever consequences resulted, were his responsibility alone. He had acknowledged that at the outset. For now he could only keep his own counsel and hope that things would turn out right in the end.

The outskirts of Farleyville passed in a blur, and he slowed the car as they approached the center of town. The shop they were heading for was located on the left at the end of a row of stores, and Grant pulled into a parking space at the side of the building.

"This is the place I was telling you about," he said as he got out of the car. "The one that specializes in American primitives."

"Oh?" Paige said as she extricated herself gracefully from the roadster, ignoring the hand Grant offered to assist her.

"Mr. Frasier has a fine collection of folk art and architechtural pieces as well as limner paintings," he continued as they approached the front door.

Paige knew the limners were the first American portraitists, house or sign painters by profession who had become itinerant artists in response to the escalating demand for decorative pieces in the late eighteenth and early nineteenth centuries. They were untrained men for the most part, and the work they produced was often stiff and out of proportion. But for all it lacked in technique and sophistication, the charm and freshness of the limner paintings endeared them to modern patrons.

A bell on the beveled-glass door tinkled a cheery welcome as they entered, and brought the shop's proprietor, a slight gray-haired man, scurrying from the back room.

"Come to buy the wee laddie, Mr. Hamilton?" he called as he came toward them. His thick Scottish brogue seemed out of place in the small heartland community.

"Not today I'm afraid, Mr. Frasier, but I've brought an expert to take a look at him. This is Miss Paige Fenton, associate conservator at the Tri-City Museum. Paige, Hannibal Frasier."

With a smile that crinkled his face from chin to hairline, the man offered her his hand. "An expert, to be sure. Well, Miss Fenton, he's a fine piece of goods, and in remarkable condition, too, considering his age." Frasier led them across the shop to a portrait hung high on the wall in what was obviously a position of honor. The painting was of a child of three or four, dressed in a suit of blue velvet, his cherubic face wreathed in a smile. In one chubby fist was clenched a painted wooden horse, as if it was his most prized possession. Paige recognized the portrait instantly as an outstanding example of limner art.

"May I?" she asked, gesturing toward the painting. Frasier nodded, and she took the picture from the wall, turning it over to examine the canvas and stretchers. She tilted it to the light to study the texture and condition of the picture's surface. "Do you have any idea who the artist might have been?"

Frasier shrugged. "It came from New England with a family that settled near Springfield. Beyond that, there's no way of knowing. The artist's anonymous like so many of those poor beggars. He probably painted this for nothing more than a winter's food and lodging."

Many limner works were unsigned, Paige knew, and were attributed to the few known artists of the period only because of similarities of style or technique.

"Well, what do you think of it, Miss Fenton?" the Scotsman queried.

"You're right, Mr. Frasier. It's a fine piece and in good condition, too, but I'd want to examine it under infrared and ultraviolet light before I'd advise Mr. Hamilton to buy it."

Frasier eyed her shrewdly. "You know your stuff, Miss Fenton," he commented.

"Thank you, Mr. Frasier."

She drifted away as the two men haggled good-naturedly over the price, an activity they'd engaged in more than once, she suspected. As Grant promised, the shop had a variety of pieces, woodwork rich with Federalist swags and dentil, weathervanes and whirligigs piled in one corner, primitive tools fashioned from both wood and metal, and needlework preserved under acetate coverings. Idly she perused the collection of samplers and mourning pictures composed of deft stitches and painted fabric. Among them she discovered a small, charming theorem painting of plump fruit and bright flowers in a wicker basket. Women of the nineteenth century had practiced the technique of using stencils on velvet to produce pictures of a certain genre, but this was a particularly fine example, with a rich and subtle use of color. It was not a museum-quality piece, yet it was lively and pleasing to the eye. Out of curiosity Paige glanced at the price.

"What did you find?" Grant inquired, peering over her shoulder.

"A very nice theorem painting, and reasonable, too," she answered, holding the square up for his approval.

He nodded appreciatively. "Why don't you let me buy it for you?" he suggested.

For a long moment she stared at him in astonishment. It would take weeks of scrimping and saving for her to buy a piece as fine as this one, and though she could not accept so costly a gift, she was touched by his offer. Then all at once she recognized his generosity for what it undoubtedly was: a bribe. Anger and disappointment boiled up in her as she placed the small painting back on the pile with the others.

"Is that the real reason you bought me antique hunting today?" she said in a tense, low voice. "Were you planning to buy me a little gift to compensate for the use of my bed and my body this morning? Or is your offer meant to be a down payment on some as yet unspecified service you want me to perform at the museum tomorrow when you meet with Arthur Franklin?"

Undaunted, she faced him, her cheeks flushed and her green eyes sparkling, magnificent in her righteous anger. While Grant cast around futilely for some way to explain, Paige continued.

"Well, your reasons don't really matter, Grant, because I can't be bought, neither my favors nor my integrity!"

Grant's own ire was beginning to glow with cold brilliance. "Oh? I've always thought," he observed caustically, "that ensuring affection and loyalty in others was as easy as determining their price. Obviously I haven't offered you enough yet, have I, Paige?" They were bitter, jaded words that revealed far more than Grant had intended, but Paige was too furious to listen.

"At least you've finally offered me something of value," she exploded.

"And what the hell do you mean by that?"

"Kisses and flowers quickly fade, but a painting is something tangible to hold on to after you're gone!"

For an instant a red haze of fury darkened Grant's vision, and it took a full minute for him to regain control.

Meanwhile Paige raged on. "I can't be bought, Grant Hamilton. Not by you, not for any price." She turned to leave the shop, but he caught her arm roughly.

"You keep accusing me of trying to buy your body and your loyalty, buy don't you have something to gain by winning my favor?"

"And just what is that?" she challenged.

"Your job maybe? Your precious position at the museum?" It was the same threat he had made that first afternoon, and it frightened her no less now. Still, she raised her head defiantly, determined not to reveal her panic.

"Let me go, Grant!" she told him frigidly, and as if by magic his hand fell away. Aware of his blazing eyes on her, Paige swept majestically out of the shop.

The rest of the afternoon was spoiled by their argument. Though they stopped at two or three other places, whatever spirit of adventure and camaraderie that existed before was gone. Still, Grant drove on stubbornly, unwilling to take Paige home.

They had been riding for the best part of an hour when Grant turned north onto the river road, away from the city.

"Just where are you taking me now?" Paige demanded, speaking the first full sentence since leaving Farleyville.

"I have something to do before I drop you off," he answered enigmatically.

A few minutes later they rolled through heavy wrought-iron gates and onto a private road that crossed a well-disciplined wooded lot and climbed steadily uphill. As they approached the flat at the crest of the bluffs, the trees fell away and an impressive French Provincial chateau came into view. Built of milky-yellow limestone indigenous to the region, it shimmered like a moonstone in the late-afternoon sun.

"What is this place?" Paige was forced to ask.

"It's Riverview, the Hamilton family homestead," Grant answered, maneuvering the car through a second set of gates that guarded the house, lawns, and gardens.

"Do you live here?" It was obvious she was impressed.

"No, this is my brother Anthony's house, by right of primogeniture. I have my own place down the hill."

As they drew up before the entry, the heavy paneled door opened, and the first honest-to-goodness butler Paige had ever seen greeted them.

"Watkins, this is Miss Fenton. Would you take her to the small sitting room and give her whatever she wants to eat and drink. I'm expecting Anthony to phone from London anytime now. I'll wait for the call in the library."

To Paige, Grant looked suddenly tense and drawn, and she watched him curiously as he headed for the double doors at the end of the foyer.

"Right this way, miss," the butler said, breaking into her thoughts. He led her through an elegant parlor and into a smaller room cozy with sunlight. "And what may I bring you?"

"Some tea would be nice," she suggested hesitantly.

"And perhaps something to go with it?" Watkins prodded.

"Yes, I'd like that." Paige realized all at once how long it had been since they had eaten breakfast. When he was gone, she explored the small, sunny chamber with its hanging plants and saffron-colored couches, its rich oriental car-

Portrait of a Lady 65

pets and gleaming mahogany furniture. Somewhere in the distance she heard a phone ringing.

When Grant came into the sitting room sometime later, Paige had finished her tea and sandwiches and was leafing through a magazine.

"Would you like something to eat or drink?" she asked, indicating the things on the silver tray. "There's lots left."

"I think I'll have a whiskey instead," he answered and headed for the table of decanters near the fireplace.

Paige addressed his back as he mixed himself a drink. "Did you have a nice chat with your brother?" she asked idly.

Grant shrugged. "We spoke about business mostly." He came to sit beside her on one of the couches, a tall drink in his hand. Judging from the color, it was far more whiskey than water, and he downed most of it in a single draught.

"Is your brother president of Hamilton Corporation?" Paige persisted for want of anything else to say.

He nodded. "And chairman of the board."

Suddenly making conversation with him was like plowing through waist-deep snow. "And do you work for him?"

Grant laughed, but without humor. "He thinks I do." He tossed off the rest of his drink and went to make another.

When he returned to the couch, his mood was miraculously altered, and he reached out to touch her face with his free hand.

"I'm sorry, Paige. When I came to your apartment this morning, I had no idea the day would turn out like this. No matter what you think, I really don't want you to compromise your position at the museum. It's just that for me there's so much more at stake than you can possibly know."

His deep-blue eyes seemed clear and earnest, but there were no real explanations behind the apology. Still, at his words, something inside her went pliable and waxen, blurring to nothingness all the harsh things they'd said that afternoon, all her questions of his intent. Paige wanted desperately to believe him, wanted to think him incapable of trying to use her to his own ends, incapable of trying to defraud the museum. But she was unsure of him. Was this an honest apology or another ploy to win her confidence and cooperation?

His fingertips moved with infinite tenderness along the line of her cheek and jaw, drawing her inexorably closer. Without the slightest struggle she succumbed to the force of his desire and the magnitude of his personality.

"Oh, Paige, I'm sorry," he whispered as his whiskey-flavored mouth closed over hers. But even as he spoke the words, she wasn't sure if he meant to beg forgiveness for past transgressions of for any betrayal the future might bring.

His kiss went to her head like the liquor itself, and she was instantly dizzy, intoxicated by the strength of her own response. She fell back helplessly against the cushions under the press of his assault, until they were lying side by side on a couch only wide enough for one. Balanced on the outside edge, Paige clung to Grant to keep from ending up on the floor, and he took full advantage of her predicament. His hands moved over her with leisurely thoroughness, cupping her hips as he pressed tight against her, touching her breasts with lingering hands, bringing her nipples erect with his stroking thumb as his kisses deepened with swelling abandon. The paths of pleasure he had explored this morning in her bed he rediscovered, making new claims on her senses until she was drowning in delight.

"Oh, Grant, I want you to make love to me," she murmured against his ear, shocked yet strangely aroused by her forwardness. "Please, please, make love to me!"

Her husky words sent molten need coursing through his veins, but he slowly shook his head. "I can't make love to you on a couch in my brother's house in broad daylight, not when the servants might come in at any minute to disturb us," he explained, laughing.

"Couldn't we lock the door?" she suggested.

"Unfortunately the doors to this room are made of glass," he told her as he came to his feet, pulling her with him.

"No, we'll have to go to my place to be alone. Here, you drive." He handed her the keys as he led her across the parlor and out the front door.

"I can't do that, Grant," she objected. "I don't know the first thing about driving a foreign car. You drive."

Grant shook his head. "I've had just enough to drink in the last few minutes, so I really shouldn't get behind the wheel. Besides, the MG works pretty much like your car except that you shift with the opposite hand."

Although he didn't seem the least bit intoxicated, she wholeheartedly supported his caution. "We could walk," she offered.

"Or go back in to the couch and chance being interrupted."

Paige acknowledged his point. "Get in the damned car, Grant," she said.

Driving the vintage MG proved to be easier than she had expected, but it took all her concentration to pilot it down the steep winding road that descended from the crest of the bluffs into the unruly copse of trees below. As they approached the bottom, a magnificent cedar-and-glass house was visible through the lush greenery. Built high on concrete pilings to keep it safe from the river's spring flooding, it seemed a fantasy house perched in the trees, its contours blending into the surrounding landscape rather than detracting from it.

They parked beside the subterranean garage and climbed steep, curving stairs to the main door. From the slate-tiled entry Paige could see across the sparsely furnished living room with its beamed ceiling to a deck and the verdant glen beyond. The base of the milky-hued bluffs rose above the trees, and a trickling stream that tumbled from the top became a waterfall that stained the rock a dusty yellow and pooled at the base to form a pond that glittered in the sunlight.

But Grant gave her no time to exclaim over the view or the house itself. He pulled her down the hallway, past the

the kitchen and bathroom, to a bedroom with austere teakwood furnishings. The late-afternoon sunlight slanting through the trees tinted the room orange, amber, and apricot, and provided an almost tangible warmth.

That warmth seemed to suffuse Paige as Grant bent to kiss her. Though his kiss was gentle at first, it grew in intensity as their tongues played and their bodies entwined. Mutual need swiftly claimed their senses, yet neither wanted to rush what was happening between them. With deliberate care Grant worked the buttons of her blouse from their buttonholes, his long fingers skimming the sensitive skin beneath. Just as provocatively she slid the shirt from his shoulders and down his arms, setting ripples of delight shuddering through him whenever her hands touched his flesh. They undressed each other slowly and with counterfeit reluctance that heightened their anticipation and the strength of their desire. At last, Grant released her hair from its confining braid and spread the rippling mass across her shoulders. She stood before him, strong and elemental, cloaked in a mantle of russet brown, and with a low moan of mingled appreciation and longing Grant took her with him to his bed.

As he lay close beside her, Paige felt his gaze move along her body, and she stared back with equal intensity. She saw how his smooth skin was gilded by the setting sun, how his dark hair and lashes glistened tawny amber, how the hard lines of his face were made abstract by the contrast of light and shadow. Without conscious thought or regret Paige stored away each impression for the inevitable time when she would be without him.

As if bound by the sultry notes and meter of some distant melody, they moved in unison, their hands stroking lazily from shoulders to flanks, their mouths melding slowly. Each gesture, each caress, was graceful, fluid, sinuous. They were willingly drugged by languorous sensation, overcome by the heady power of lingering kisses, until a swelling urgency that was too strong and too persistent to deny took hold.

For an instant Grant turned away to take the most basic precautions and then returned to her, ready, virile, and eager. They came together with agonizing slowness, Grant's body flowing along the length of hers, his rugged symmetry a perfect foil for the complex curves that were the essence of her femininity.

Their eyes held with wonder and trust as waves of bliss rolled over them. Their bodies merged with greater tenderness and intimacy with each gentle stroke, and around them their world went loose and fluid, pale and melting. Their senses diffused as they reached their crescendo so that no single perception could be isolated or believed. Everything rushed together in a swirling kaleidoscope of impressions and sensations, then slowly ebbed away, receding like the outgoing tide with ripples of delight returning and returning and returning. But at last the delight returned no more, and they drifted to sleep, exhausted and sated.

When Paige awoke sometime later, the sunset that had filled the room with vibrant color was nothing more than a stain on the horizon. In the semi-dark she could barely make out the man beside her, his features hollow and indistinct as he lay with one arm and one leg draped possessively over her. Since Grant held her immobile, she had no choice but to watch him as he slept.

How unpredictable and complex a man he was, she mused. How changeable, inconsistent, demanding. His moods, whatever caused them, were swiftly over and forgotten, his flares of temper blindingly bright and quickly burned away. His humor was wry and unaffected, his manner with others easygoing and sincere. She tried to tally all she knew about him and found the sum frustratingly small. She had no understanding of Grant on which to base her feelings, yet she had fallen in love with him. It was a folly she was sure to regret, and still she was irresistibly drawn to him. Though she wasn't sure what Grant really was, she was very aware of what he might be: a forger, defrauder, playboy, roué. Yet even that knowledge could not save her from him.

"Oh, please, please, please," she whispered beseechingly into the darkness as tears tracked into her hair. But even as she said the words, she wasn't sure just what it was she wanted.

CHAPTER
Six

FROM THE SET of his firm mouth and the way he toyed with his pen, it was obvious to Paige that Grant was nervous. The realization did strange things to her insides. Sitting alone on the far side of the long table in the conference room adjacent to Arthur Franklin's office, he seemed hopelessly outnumbered as the art museum personnel began to file into the room. There was Director Franklin at the head of the table, places reserved for Evan Rogers and Paige herself, and to her left six of Tri-City's seven curators and four curatorial assistants who had come to hear Evan's findings. Though she was not privy to the results of the tests, she knew they would not bode well for Grant's cause.

Paige had been *persona non grata* in the lab this morning as Evan was concluding his tests on "The Lady of Dordrect," and though she resented being shut out, she understood his concern about compromising her position in the controversy over the painting. Within the close-knit art world, where subjective judgments were the rule and not the exception, a connoisseur, conservator, or curator's reputation must be above reproach. Though academic prowess carried substantial weight, often one's entire career hinged on the intangible credibility built up over the years.

Paige had put her reputation on the line when she challenged the authenticity of "The Lady of Dordrect," but she'd clearly had no choice. She would have been derelict in her duty to the museum if she hadn't brought the matter to light. In more ways than one, the disclosures of the next minutes would decide her future. And it was only since she had come to know and love Grant that she realized how high a price she might be forced to pay for professional vindication.

Nor had the activity with which she'd chosen to keep herself occupied while the tests were being run done much for her peace of mind. Filing yellowed newspaper articles, crumpled letters, and musty souvenirs from Tri-City's early days for the museum's archivist should have been good therapy, but plump, middle-aged Madeline Pryor had been in the mood for gossip. As Paige had feared, the incident with Grant on the dance floor at Arthur Franklin's party and their sudden disappearance afterward had caused tongues to wag. And Madeline had wanted to know all the details. Paige's replies had been polite and noncommittal, but the other woman's curiosity was not appeased.

"Well, I wouldn't get mixed up with Grant Hamilton if I were you," she advised. Although Paige bent diligently over the folder she was filing in an attempt to convey a total disinterest in Grant's past, Madeline forged on undeterred. "He's had a reputation for fast living for as long as I can remember, and his marriage to a society girl from back East didn't slow him down much. She was a real beauty and from old money, too. Of course, the public relations job his father gave him out at Hamilton Corporation couldn't have helped much. He was traveling all over the world, having

Portrait of a Lady

his picture in the newspaper with one celebrity or another, and always with some gorgeous girl draped all over him. Anyway, when his wife filed for a divorce, it was easy to guess the grounds."

"Really, Madeline," Paige interrupted, "I don't care to hear about Grant Hamilton's escapades. What he was doing a few years ago has very little bearing on the fact that I danced with him on Friday night and accepted his help when I locked the keys in my car."

The older woman seemed hurt by Paige's curt reply. "Well, I was only telling you all this for your own good, my dear," Madeline sulked. "Grant Hamilton is a good-looking and charming man, but he's also wild, unpredictable, and reckless. They say he nearly killed himself some years back by driving off Bluff Road and into the river one night after a drunken party! So be careful with him, Paige. You're a good, sensible girl, and I'd hate to see you get hurt. Now, if it was Anthony Hamilton who'd caught your eye, I'd say 'good for you.' He's a fine man and a pillar of this community, not at all like his brother."

Paige knew Grant far better than Madeline Pryor did, she reasoned as she sat a scant yard from the subject of this morning's discussions, and she had far more insight into his character. Still, the revelations of Grant's past and the older woman's warnings weighed on her mind. Couldn't a man capable of the misdeeds Madeline Pryor had disclosed be unscrupulous enough to try to deceive the museum? It was a long step from adultery to fraud, but couldn't a man willing to cheat on his wife try to cheat the rest of the world, too? Paige just wasn't sure.

Precisely at two o'clock, Evan Rogers bustled into the conference room, and Paige knew that the answers to at least some of her questions were at hand.

Franklin immediately opened the meeting by introducing Grant to Evan Rogers and the rest of the staff. "Since Mr. Rogers needs to catch a three-thirty plane, I think we should be brief." He continued. "We all know why we're here, so,

Evan, please explain your findings."

The small man beside Paige opened a manila folder, put on his reading glasses, and cleared his throat. "The tests I was asked to run on 'The Lady of Dordrect,' allegedly painted by Frans Hals about 1650, were to establish the painting's authenticity. To that end I conducted an evaluation that included physical, microscopic, X-ray, and chemical analyses of the work. From the results of those tests, I can state beyond the shadow of a doubt that 'The Lady of Dordrect' is a forgery."

Grant went pale beneath his tan but sat calmly, obviously determined to assimilate every scrap of evidence that condemned "The Lady of Dordrect" as a fake. Paige listened with equal intensity, evaluating and interpreting Evan's findings for herself.

Someone had obviously gone to a great deal of trouble to make the painting appear genuine. The canvas and stretchers were authentic seventeenth-century pieces; the pigments were hand ground, prepared in the manner Hals would have used, and true to the period. The artist even used badger-hair brushes to paint the portrait.

Yet as skillful as the forger was, there were elements he could not control. Paint matures and oxidizes over the centuries in ways that cannot be counterfeited. The freshness of the pigments beneath the yellowing coat of varnish had first made Paige suspicious of the painting. In the end those intangible factors proved "The Lady" was not all she seemed. The pattern of tiny fissures and lines that formed in the paint surface during normal aging—the craquelure—was too sharp and jagged to have been caused by gradual drying, and the accumulation of dust in these crevices was too uniform to have built up slowly over the years. These things could be seen readily under a microscope, but only if an art expert had reason to look for them. Any technical examination done on a piece as well known and as well documented as "The Lady of Dordrect" would be cursory at best.

"In conclusion," Evan Rogers summed up, "'The Lady

of Dordrect' is a painting done on three-hundred-year-old canvas with materials, techniques, and brushes contemporary to that period. But regardless, the portrait is undoubtedly of modern origin."

There was a resounding moment of silence as Evan's pronouncement sank in before anyone spoke.

"So, 'The Lady' is a forgery after all," Grant mused, as much to himself as to the others at the long conference table.

Rogers nodded. "It's a very good forgery, to be sure, with a technique that rivals Hals's own. My guess is that it was painted prior to World War II by someone who had studied Dutch and Flemish art extensively and had access to genuine works by the master. No doubt the forger used solvents such as phenol and formaldehyde to make the paint dry faster, baked the work to enhance the craquelure, and dusted it with something to simulate a collection of dirt."

"But 'The Lady of Dordrect' has been in the family since the late eighteen hundreds," Grant pointed out, his tone sharp. "And what about all the documentation we have for the portrait: bills of sale, lists of previous owners, certificates of authentication? Don't they mean anything? Then, too, Phillip Argenta inspected the painting just prior to the sale and assured us it was genuine. He's one of the world's foremost experts on Hals. Was he wrong about 'The Lady'?"

Franklin sighed. "I think the results of Evan's tests prove he was. Unfortunately, Mr. Argenta is traveling in Europe, and we haven't been able to get in touch with him. As you might imagine, I'm very anxious to discuss this matter with him."

"Perhaps the extensive provenance for the work indicates that at some point a genuine 'Lady of Dordrect' was sold while your family retained an excellent copy, Mr. Hamilton," Rogers suggested.

"No one else in my family would ever have agreed to sell 'The Lady,'" Grant snapped back coldly. "Besides, if that were so, wouldn't all the documentation have been passed on with the original? And why doesn't the art world know about a duplicate 'Lady of Dordrect' if there is one?"

Evan Rogers receded into his high-backed chair. "I was only indulging in some speculation, gentlemen. It seems that 'The Lady of Dordrect' is like so many females: The more we come to know about her, the deeper her mystery. Now, if you will excuse me, I have a plane to catch."

With Evan's departure the meeting drew to a close. One by one the curators and their assistants shuffled their papers and rose to return to their offices, leaving Arthur Franklin, Grant, and Paige seated at one end of the table.

"Well, Director Franklin," Grant finally began, "where does this leave us? Considering the real age of the portrait, it's obvious I didn't have the work painted to deliberately defraud the museum."

"That's true," the gray-haired man conceded, "but it doesn't absolve you of trying to sell a painting you knew to be a forgery."

Grant's intimidating brows lowered, and his eyes glittered like shards of broken glass. "Are you going to bring charges, then?"

There was a resonant pause while the director took the measure of the younger man. Paige found she was holding her breath as she waited for his answer. "No, at least not for the moment. Should we find any discrepancies in the other pieces that were offered for sale along with the Hals portrait, we might be forced to change our minds, but the museum doesn't want to turn this into a scandal any more than Hamilton Corporation does."

"At least we're in agreement on that," Grant replied, his eyes still flinty.

"Then perhaps there's one more thing you'd be willing to do before you return to your office," Franklin suggested.

"What's that?"

"When Evan gave me the preliminary report on the painting, I scheduled a press conference for this afternoon. Since we intended to use 'The Lady of Dordrect' as a centerpiece for the show that opens Friday, I felt it was necessary to break this news as soon as possible so it will not detract from the Northern Light exhibition. I'd like you to be at the press conference with me."

Paige saw Grant's forehead crease. Obviously he didn't relish meeting the press on this matter, but it seemed he had no choice.

"I suppose you have a statement of some sort prepared for the media?" Grant inquired, and Franklin nodded. "Well, then, if I can see one of the press releases and have a few minutes alone to prepare my reply to it, I'll be willing to stay."

"Very well," Franklin agreed, smiling. He indicated the adjoining room. "Feel free to use my office, Mr. Hamilton. The statement I'm planning to read is on my desk. Help yourself to anything you need."

As Grant closed the door behind him, Franklin turned to Paige. "I want you at the press conference, too," he told her. "After all, you were the one who first discovered the forgery, and deserve full credit for the disclosure. I'd also like someone to field any technical questions that might arise."

"Yes, sir," she agreed reluctantly as she gathered up the report Evan had left spread across the table. The thought of facing the press herself, combined with the suspicion that Grant was about to be thrown to the wolves, sent icy dread coursing through her. With all her heart she wished she'd played no role in this debacle.

The reporters were gathered in a noisy clump in the front rows of the small auditorium when Grant, Director Franklin, and Paige came onto the stage. Two chairs flanked a podium in the center, and a sheet-draped painting on an easel stood beyond. As they took their places, Paige and Grant on the chairs and Franklin at the microphone, Paige let her gaze drift over to where Grant was sitting. In his dark business suit, pale-blue shirt, and club tie he looked calm, powerful, and totally in control. Her eyes moved over him—his hair rich brown without the sun to burnish its golden streaks, his profile resolute and strong. She had heard the reports on "The Lady of Dordrect," had seen his reaction to them, and still she didn't know if he was guilty or innocent of deception.

"Ladies and gentlemen of the press," Franklin said, calling the group to order, "you have been invited here today because, in preparing a new museum acquisition for display, one of our conservators discovered, and subsequent tests have proved, that the work 'The Lady of Dordrect,' allegedly painted by Frans Hals, is a forgery."

There was a murmur of excited voices as pens and pencils worked in unison, taking notes. Someone asked how to spell "Dordrect," and Franklin complied. Judging from the change in their demeanor, this was a far more important story than any of the newspeople had anticipated. They listened with rapt attention as Franklin read the prepared statement outlining the discovery of the forgery and the tests that proved the allegations, as well as a brief history of the portrait. Then the director turned the podium and microphone over to Grant, who spoke extemporaneously with a poise and presence that instantly won over his listeners.

"Speaking for both the Hamilton family and Hamilton Corporation, I want to express my deep regret for this incident. When we offered 'The Lady of Dordrect' to the Tri-City Art Museum, it was with the hope that each new generation of museum-goers would come to enjoy and appreciate an exemplary piece of art painted by a master of a bygone era. To find now, after all the years that 'The Lady of Dordrect' has been treasured by my family, that the portrait is not all it seems shocks and saddens me. My regret is not for myself, the Hamilton family, the Tri-City Museum, or even the greater Tri-City area, but for the art world at large. In the discovery that has been made today we have forfeited an historic link with our artistic past."

Grant's words, so appropriate and sincerely delivered, brought a warm swell of pride to Paige's chest, and she had to swallow hard when Arthur Franklin called her to the podium. Once she was before the lights and cameras, her nervousness dissolved, and her lecture-hall manner took over. She explained clearly and concisely how she had become suspicious of the painting's origins, then elaborated on the tests done to determine the portrait's authenticity. Finally Franklin opened the floor to questions, and a dozen voices clamored for recognition.

"Will this discovery affect the opening of the Northern Light show scheduled for Friday?" someone asked and received a negative answer. "Will other works donated by the Hamilton Corporation be suspect as a result of this discovery?" Again Franklin said no, though Paige knew that wasn't the whole truth.

"Are criminal charges going to be brought against Mr. Hamilton for attempting to defraud the museum?" a bushy-haired reporter in a rumpled sports jacket wanted to know.

Arthur Franklin frowned. "At the moment we are not quite sure how the Hamilton family came to possess a counterfeit Hals portrait, and since Mr. Hamilton offered the painting to us in good faith, no charges will be brought."

"Was the acquisition of 'The Lady of Dordrect' a donation or a purchase?" someone asked. "And if it was a purchase, how much was the Tri-City Museum prepared to pay for the painting?"

"'The Lady of Dordrect' was to have been purchased from the Hamilton family in conjunction with a number of other works for a price I am not at liberty to divulge," Franklin answered smoothly and moved on, unwilling, as most museum administrators were, to discuss the worth of new acquisitions or pieces already owned by their institutions.

"Just why are you selling off your family's extensive collection of art and antiques, Mr. Hamilton?" a sharp-eyed female reporter in the first row called out.

Grant stepped to the microphone, his expression serious. "We're by no means selling all our art and antiques," he began. "What this sale does represent is a shift in both family and corporate policy toward a gradual dispersal of these pieces. It is our belief that the days of huge private art collections are numbered. Along with encouraging new talent and working to preserve significant arts and crafts from the past, the duty of a responsible art patron is to share his treasures with the rest of the world. The sale of these pieces, including 'The Lady of Dordrect,' to the Tri-City Museum represents a step toward putting that philosophy into practice."

"And I suppose the sale has nothing to do with the rumors that Hamilton Corporation is in deep financial trouble as a result of the cancellation of those defense contracts last spring?" the same woman persisted.

"The rumors you refer to are groundless. As a matter of fact, Hamilton Corporation is expanding. We are building a new plant at Shale Valley, and I believe that when my brother returns from Europe, we may well have an announcement that will have a favorable effect on the local economy. By selling portions of the Hamilton family collection to the Tri-City Art Museum we intend to share our communal artistic heritage."

"If your interest is indeed so philanthropic, Mr. Hamilton," someone called out, "why didn't you donate rather than sell the artwork?" The pointed question was meant to put Grant on the defensive, but he diffused its malicious intent with an easy laugh and wry grin.

"I guess because neither Hamilton Corporation nor the Hamilton family can afford to be quite that generous," he replied truthfully.

A few more questions followed, but they were innocuous for the most part, and afterward Arthur Franklin unveiled the portrait propped up on its easel and allowed the photographers and cameramen free access to the painting. As the posing and picture-taking subsided and the reporters packed up their notebooks, cameras, and other gear, Grant sidled over to where Paige was standing.

"We still have a dinner date for this evening, don't we?" he reminded her softly.

The casual comment he'd made Friday night came immediately to mind, and Paige turned wide, searching eyes on him. "You mustn't feel compelled to honor that commitment, Grant," she assured him bravely. "After what's happened, you surely aren't in the mood to spend the evening with me."

Now that he no longer had a reason to seek her favor, Paige was willing to give him the opportunity to escape both their evening together and the burgeoning relationship between them. Yet with all her heart she hoped Grant would elect to stay with her.

Warm, vital fingers slid compellingly around her wrist, and even in the auditorium where anyone might see and read her expression, Paige's eyes lit with eager response to his touch.

"On the contrary, Paige," he replied in an undertone, "the thought of being with you tonight is the only thing that makes the rest of this day bearable. I'll pick you up at your place at about seven-thirty."

He relinquished his hold on her with a delicious reluctance that left Paige weak. Wanting desperately to believe every word he'd said, she stared after him as he strode up the aisle and disappeared out the doors at the rear of the auditorium.

At a corner table in Lee Gow's, the area's finest Chinese restaurant, Paige sat eating her sizzling rice soup with a diligence that had little to do with assuaging her hunger, while Grant at her side stared absently into space between spoonfuls. Only the most cursory comments had passed between them since they were seated, and even those had dealt primarily with items on the menu. They might have been strangers sharing a table in the crowded establishment except for the furtive, sidelong glances Paige cast him. Concern shone in her eyes, but she seemed unable to articulate her feelings and took refuge in the meal before her.

Finally Grant broke the taut silence. "May I have a bit more soup, please?" he inquired, indicating the tureen at her elbow.

Paige started at the sound of his voice, raised in even so mundane a request, and she hurried to ladle soup into his bowl. She returned to her own dinner as soon as she had completed the task, but as he watched her, a frown began to gather on Grant's brow.

"Dammit, Paige," he swore softly, "I admit I'm not very happy that 'The Lady of Dordrect' turned out to be a forgery, but I don't hold you personally responsible for it. You needn't spend the evening cowering, as if you expected me to beat you." His frown deepened in exasperation when she still refused to look at him. "Don't you understand that one of the reasons I wanted to spend tonight with you was to help celebrate your victory? Aren't you pleased that you won, that the tests on 'The Lady' came out in your favor?"

Slowly she raised her eyes to his face. "There was never any question in my mind as to how this would turn out, Grant, so I don't see any cause for celebration. I knew all along what the tests would prove. I'm just sorry that, because I won, you had to lose."

Paige hoped she hadn't revealed too much about her feelings for him. She had indeed redeemed herself at the museum and preserved her credibility in the art world, but the price had been very dear. She turned back to her soup with feigned relish so that Grant wouldn't guess how much she regretted her victory, or see the tears that glazed her eyes.

"Well, at least what happened this afternoon proved that I wanted no concessions from you," he persisted. It was evident that her accusations about his motives had stung, and Paige experienced a swift surge of remorse. "I didn't

Portrait of a Lady

ask for your help, did I? I didn't expect you to compromise your position at the museum for my sake. Surely you can see that you were wrong, that what happened between us this weekend had nothing to do with 'The Lady of Dordrect.'"

Paige set down her spoon and watched him earnestly. "No, you didn't ask for concessions, I admit. But in spite of all that's happened, nothing has proved that you didn't know 'The Lady of Dordrect' was a forgery when you sold it to the museum." Paige hated herself for voicing the doubt, but she couldn't rest until that last question was resolved between them.

Grant glared at her, his eyes narrowed. "How can you have so little faith in me?" he exploded. "Have I given you cause to doubt me? By God, Paige, you expect a lot from a man! If I swore that I had no inkling that 'The Lady of Dordrect' was a fake when I offered it for sale, would you even believe me?"

How unfair she was being, if he was indeed telling the truth, Paige realized suddenly. Yet she was compelled to resolve her suspicions before she could open herself to him more completely. "Oh, Grant, I want so much to believe you—"

What she had been about to say was abruptly abbreviated by the arrival of the next course. With nimble ease the waiter cleared away their soup bowls, poured a thin brown sauce over pot stickers, and set the platter of wonton-wrapped dumplings between them.

When the man was gone, Grant began to speak in a low tone. "Have I given you cause to doubt me, Paige?" he repeated. His piercing blue gaze raked her face, as if he intended to read her answer in her expression, in her eyes, in the pores of her skin. Then recognition flickered in the midnight-dark pupils, and he moved closer. "At least some of this doubt lies in the fact that someone has seen fit to warn you against me, doesn't it?" he accused.

Paige felt a flush color her cheeks, and she knew she couldn't deny that the rumors had played a part in deepening her mistrust of him.

"Did they tell you my whole life story or just the juicy parts?"

Not knowing how to answer him, she stared helplessly at her plate, ashamed to admit she had listened to gossip, but aware too that her doubts ran far deeper than the things Madeline Pryor had disclosed.

"Did you hear that I've been wild and reckless and ran with the 'wrong' companions most of my life? Did they say I've caused more than my share of scandals? Well, there's a gram of truth in that!" The insistent note of self-mockery made Paige glance up at him in surprise.

But as she sat watching him in silence, simply waiting for him to continue, Grant found in her wide, soft eyes a potent antidote for the old doubts and insecurities that still had the power to overwhelm and confuse him. Her need to understand was a balm for his pride, and when he spoke again, his voice was calmer, cooler, more conversational.

"I suppose you heard that when I married it was because the girl was carrying my child," he began. "At the time I thought it was the only thing to do—to drop out of college to provide for Linda and the baby. They were my responsibility, both financially and socially, and I was anxious to prove I was capable of caring for them. When I left school, I expected that my father would take me into Hamilton Corporation as he had Anthony a few years before."

"Didn't he?" Paige asked.

Grant sipped from the tiny handleless teacup, the delicate porcelain dwarfed by his large, capable hand. "Oh, I had my place in the company, all right. But it wasn't in the business end, like the position he'd offered Anthony, or even as a research assistant, as I had hoped. No, my job was in public relations, where I couldn't screw up or do any real harm. I didn't argue with Dad about it; I had a wife and child to support, after all. So I dutifully played in dozens of tennis matches and golf tournaments, raced Hamilton Corporation-sponsored speedboats and stock cars all over the United States. To be fair to my father, sports were the only place he'd ever seen me excel, and he thought he had offered me a job that suited my capabilities. But I hated being a corporate mascot and resented being denied a chance to develop my other talents."

"Why would any man do that to his son?" Paige murmured, trying to grapple with the complexities of the man beside her. The pause grew protracted as she waited for an answer, and Grant shrugged uncomfortably, trying to sidestep the question. But having glimpsed another layer of feeling beneath his veneer of calm and polish, beneath his casual cynicism and glib indifference, she pressed him until he began to explain.

What emerged was a portrait of a boy growing up in a home where his abilities ran counter to those valued by his own family. His insatiable interest in what made things work had led him to a series of seedy garages and later to Hamilton Corporation's own workshops and hangars, where his restless curiosity could be appeased. While he developed his understanding and skills with mechanical things, he also grew to have, as his mother had put it, "an appalling penchant for dirt and the lower classes."

Paige sensed that things had not been easy when Grant was growing up, since he was trying to buy the love and respect of his family with foreign coin. In those formative years his athletic prowess had been the only common medium of exchange, and through his performance on the athletic field he had sought to secure his family's acceptance. All at once Paige began to understand the forces that had tempered and formed Grant Hamilton into the man he was.

"What about your wife and child?" Paige finally asked.

Grant pursed his lips, then sighed; none of the answers she wanted were easy ones. "The baby was premature and survived only a few days," he said quietly. "Though we both really tried, our marriage didn't stand much of a chance after that. I was on the road a lot and living a pretty fast life; Linda was bored here and missed her family and friends back East. Things just deteriorated without a baby to hold us together, and I think both of us were relieved when the divorce was final."

His sapphire eyes came to rest on Paige's face, pale and creamy in the warm light cast by the ornate brass lanterns that hung from the ceiling. He had expected her expression to be judgmental, but it was calm and impassive, as if she were simply waiting for him to continue. In her eyes he saw sincere interest and gentle compassion, and suddenly he understood that he had only to be truthful to win her acceptance.

He shook his head slowly as he continued. "I'm not particularly proud of what happened after that. I just let myself get caught up in the momentum of what I was doing: sports all day, drinking and women all night. It was a pretty decadent life, the kind rich boys are supposed to enjoy. So I gave it my best. And then one night I drove off Bluff Road and into the river."

"How did it happen?" Paige pressed him when he would have let the subject drop.

Grant glanced past her as if caught up in the memory. "I had been to a party at the Elmgrove Country Club and left just before dawn. To this day I don't know why I fastened my seat belt when I left the club, but that's what saved me. One minute I was driving along the road up by Carlyle Point, and the next I was in the river." He gave a hollow laugh. "It's amazing how lucid you suddenly become when you're trapped in a car sinking in thirty feet of water. Just as promised, my whole life flashed before me, and I was appalled by how little I'd accomplished. It's pretty melodramatic, but I swore if I got out of the river alive, I'd straighten things out and make something of myself."

Unconsciously Paige covered his hand with hers. "What happened?" she asked in a whisper.

"I knew in theory that when the car was nearly filled

with water, the pressure would equalize, and I'd be able to force the door open. It was agonizing, but I waited, took a last gulp of air, and pushed. Thank God, the theory worked, and I swam for the surface, ending up with only a few cuts and bruises to show for the experience. But those few minutes in the river changed me in a hundred ways that didn't show.

"When I asked my father for a change of position at Hamilton Corporation, he refused me, so I went back to school, determined to become an expert in avionics. It was a relatively new field then, using electronics and computers for airplane navigation, communication, and so on. It was one I knew Hamilton Corporation was investigating. After I'd completed my degrees, I went to work for the family's largest competitor, since I knew there was no place for me in my father's company. At Air-Tech I was on a team that developed a whole new process for determining in-flight positions, and that success was all the sweeter for having earned it on my own."

"But how did you return to Hamilton Corporation?" Paige asked.

"When the news of our breakthrough became public, my father called me and offered me the job of corporate research coordinator at Hamilton Corporation, and I took it." Despite Grant's simple declaration, understated and restrained, there was a note of deep pride in his voice, and Paige realized how much that call must have meant to him. At last he had been accepted by his family for what he was.

"Though I still have an office in the research section, I rarely get to use it," he went on. "I spend most of my time presenting the findings that come out of our labs to corporate management and to the government, to keep up the level of funding for our development teams."

"And do you like your job?" Paige wondered aloud.

An odd expression crossed his strong features as he belatedly turned his attention to the platter of cooling appetizers sitting untouched between them. "For the most part."

As Grant nibbled on the pot stickers, Paige's mind was busy. The things he had confided tonight explained so much: why he'd been as careful about contraception as she, why he drank so seldomly, and why he'd been so adamant about not driving the single time she'd seen him indulge. At last she was beginning to understand, too, Grant's strange, convoluted relationship with his brother. If his characterization of himself as he had been a dozen years earlier was even remotely correct, Paige suddenly realized how far he'd come on nothing more than his own determination. Another man might have allowed himself to drift in a sea of luxury and self-indulgence, but Grant had proved his strength and independence the hard way.

Her heart warmed to him with the insight, and she found her suspicions about him falling away. No man who had fought so long and hard for the respect of his family and associates would jeopardize all he'd won on a scheme to defraud the museum. And if he had no knowledge that "The Lady of Dordrect" was a forgery, he had no reason to counterfeit his feelings for her either.

With that realization, sweet serenity seeped through her veins. In a totally uncharacteristic gesture Paige leaned across to give him a warm, provocative kiss that left them both a little flushed and giddy. Surprised and confused by the sudden change in her, Grant sat grinning, suddenly at ease with her and the things she'd encouraged him to reveal.

Since it was meant to be shared, the Chinese food made for a companionable meal. Though Grant had ordered far more than they could possibly eat, they approached the dinner with relish. There were plump pink shrimp in a delicate lobster sauce, spicy Szechuan beef, and cashew chicken with succulent meat, crispy vegetables, and nuts. At the table their waiter assembled moo shu pork—thin rice pancakes spread with a coating of plum sauce and a filling of shredded pork and vegetables, all skillfully wrapped by a pair of deftly flying chopsticks. A steaming bowl of snowy rice and another pot of hot tea completed the meal, and they freely indulged themselves, exclaiming over the medley of flavors and textures, delighting in the meal and the companionship.

For the first time the constraint between them vanished. Grant had bravely faced the truth about "The Lady of Dordrect," and Paige had finally found a reason to believe him innocent of any duplicity. They were free at last to be nothing more than what they were: a man and woman caught up in their mutual attraction. As the meal progressed, there was an easy camaraderie between them: their eyes meeting as they shared an observation or a joke, their hands brushing as they passed dishes back and forth, their moods totally attuned. The banter between them was lighthearted and gay, with Grant's smile flashing in appreciation of her comments and Paige's laugh rippling up from deep inside. An aura of contentment surrounded them, bathing them in mellow, golden light.

When at last they sat back sated, the waiter cleared away their dishes and then returned to put a plate of fortune cookies between them.

"You first." Grant gestured toward the two folded cookies.

"Afraid?" Paige challenged, grinning, her fingers poised over the pair as if her fate really did depend on which one she chose.

"No, just polite. Take your pick."

She selected the one on the left and snapped it open. Grant endured the dramatic pause as she withdrew the slender strip of paper and shot him a look fraught with meaning. Clearing her throat, she read the message: "Good fortune sometimes wears a mysterious disguise." Paige frowned. "What do you suppose that means?"

Grant's warm fingers closed over hers in an attempt to capture the small slip of paper. "I think it means you got my fortune by mistake," he suggested pointedly.

"Oh?" Paige's green eyes were shining, and she was intensely aware of his nearness. "Why do you say that?"

His voice was velvety, and his hand had tightened around hers in a masterful caress. "As catastrophic as it's been to discover that 'The Lady' is a forgery, some good has come of it. It brought you to me."

Tenderness seemed to melt through Paige, leaving her warm and trusting. "And do you consider meeting me such good fortune?" she wanted to know.

"What do you think, Paige?" Grant teased. His ravishing gaze moved over her, along the curve of her pink-tinged cheek to her smiling lips, across the turning of her jaw, and down her alabaster throat to the deep V where the silky blue-gray dress pulled taut across her breasts. His eyes slowly reversed their path, and when they returned to meet hers, they were dark and smoky with desire.

Her body warmed in response, as if it had been his hands and not his eyes that had run so freely over her. How was it Grant could make her ache with longing without so much as a touch passing between them? Paige drew a deep breath to try to clear her head, but her thoughts were full of making love to him.

"I think you should stop quibbling over whose fortune is whose and open that cookie." Her tone was husky and filled with promise.

Grant grinned and snatched the remaining cookie from the plate. With a snap he broke the confection in half and put one of the pieces in his mouth while he read the message. His lips thinned, drawing into a harsh line that marred his expression as his eyes moved over the words a second time.

Aware of a change in him, but at a loss to explain it, Paige prodded him impatiently. "Well, what is it? What does it say? Aren't you going to read your fortune to me?"

Grant's expression was vague, as if he wasn't sure who she was. "No," he said simply.

Paige couldn't have been more stunned if he had shouted

the word. Gone was the gentle camaraderie and easy banter, the warm communication and simmering sexuality that had existed between them only moments before. His chameleon-like transformation left her bereft, shaken, and confused. As she grappled with the sudden change in him and tried to fathom its cause, Grant rose to stand over her, carelessly stripped bills from a wad of money he took from his pocket, and tossed them on the table.

As they sped back through the darkened streets toward Conway Park, Paige tried to make sense out of Grant's behavior. What had been in his fortune to upset him so? For the most part the sayings were ambiguous enough to be applied to any circumstances, and Grant was certainly not superstitious. Still, it was obvious something had struck a responsive chord in him, and Paige wished desperately that she knew what the fortune had said.

Not a word passed between them on the ride home, and when he walked her to the door, Paige stood staring up into his dark face, wondering at his thoughts.

"I could make a pot of coffee if you'd like to come in and talk," she offered hopefully.

His eyes were icy and remote, and even before he said the words, Paige knew that he was going to shut her out completely. "I'm sorry if I've been less than attentive, Paige, but I do have a great deal on my mind tonight."

It was an empty excuse for the change in his behavior, but it was all the explanation or apology he seemed willing to offer. Following his lead, Paige said a hasty good night and with a helpless gesture turned to go inside. As she climbed the stairs to her apartment, she hoped Grant would change his mind and follow her. But when she secured the door behind her, she was left alone with her doubts and confusion.

Grant waited out front until he saw the lights come on in Paige's windows, then reached into his pocket for the car keys. His fingers encountered the slender slip of paper that had cast a pall on an otherwise wonderful evening. By the light of the street lamp he reread the treacherous words—"Secrets have the power to jeopardize all you hold dear"—and once more he was engulfed by the same terrible foreboding that had overwhelmed him in the restaurant.

In his own mind there was no question about what the fortune meant. When he had talked to Anthony on Sunday, he had deliberately kept the controversy over "The Lady of Dordrect" to himself, and now he doubted the wisdom of his decision. Would this secret further strain the already tenuous relationship between him and his brother? He had also kept his own counsel in dealing with the situation at the museum, rather than consulting Hamilton Corporation's board of directors or the company's lawyers for advice, and he couldn't help but wonder if that omission could threaten his position there. Was it possible that the publicity resulting from the museum's findings might jeopardize all they had been working to prevent? The fortune had abruptly reminded him of just how much was at stake, and the dread that had been simmering inside him ever since the painting's authenticity had been questioned had suddenly boiled over.

Grant drew a deep breath and inserted his key in the car's ignition. Tomorrow morning Anthony would return from Europe in triumph, with newly negotiated contracts in hand, while Grant would have to admit his failure and face the consequences of keeping his secrets. The thought of his brother's inevitable recriminations was a grim one that had quickly banished more frivolous concerns from his mind.

Yet he was genuinely sorry his restive mood had spoiled the evening with Paige. She was as enchanting a woman as he had ever met, and he was growing increasingly fond of her. For a moment he let himself dwell on her depth and intelligence, her beauty and innate sexuality, and he wished he had been able to explain both his fortune and its ramifications. But that would have forced him to divulge information he could not share. Distractedly he ran his fingers through his tousled hair. He'd just have to find a way to make this up to her, he decided.

For now his mind was too occupied with thoughts of the morning's confrontation to consider much else. With a single backward glance at Paige's lighted windows, Grant gunned the car's engine and drove off into the night.

CHAPTER
Seven

FOR WHAT MUST have been the tenth time in the past hour the shrill jangling of the telephone interrupted Paige's concentration. With a murmur of exasperation she turned from the nineteenth-century etching she had been examining to pick up the receiver. It was another reporter. Judging from the number and caliber of the calls she'd received today, art forgeries like "The Lady of Dordrect" were big news. By noon Paige had talked to people from newspapers and magazines all across the country, including *The New York Times*, *U.S.A. Today*, and *Art News*. Rumor had it that reporters from a couple of morning news programs had called Arthur Franklin, but he didn't mention it when they met with local TV reporters just after lunch.

Paige did not enjoy acting as a spokesperson for the museum, but the fact that the media seemed determined to

Portrait of a Lady

cast her in the role of "giant killer" distressed her most. Though she knew the reporters were only trying to add depth and interest to their news stories, their insistence that she was trying to bring down Hamilton Corporation by slinging accusations was one she could not countenance. The last thing she wanted was to endanger the long-standing relationship between Hamilton Corporation and the Tri-City Museum. It was with marked relief that Paige saw the cameramen douse their lights and put away their equipment at last. And in spite of the way they had parted the previous night, Paige couldn't help but wonder how Grant was handling this flood of publicity at his end.

Somewhat later, Arthur Franklin came into the conservation lab. Paige motioned him to a chair while she completed her telephone conversation with a features writer from Wichita. Something about Franklin's precise, spare movements set Paige's nerves on edge, and she concluded the call as quickly as possible.

"Has today been as crazy here as it's been in my office?" he asked as she replaced the receiver. "My secretary says if she gets one more call from someone with a genuine Hals stashed in the attic, she's going to buy it herself and retire on the profit she'll make when she sells it back to us."

Paige laughed. "That sounds like Marcella. I've been transferring calls like that to Caroline Lyons. After all, she's the curator of European painting; she's the one those people should talk to if they have a newly discovered Hals for sale."

Franklin's answering chuckle was perfunctory and short-lived. With a vague, dismissing gesture he rose from his chair to pace the near end of the lab. "Paige," he began at last, "this is one of the hardest things I've ever had to do as director of this museum. I want you to understand that I wouldn't do it at all if I had my choice in the matter."

Paige watched him expectantly, a hollow feeling in her middle.

"Just a few minutes ago I had a call from Mr. Hamilton

out at Hamilton Corporation. Apparently they have been deluged with calls today, too. He's furious about all the negative publicity that's been generated by the situation, and he's demanding concessions. He wants your job, Paige; he wants you fired from your position here at the museum."

For a few moments Paige could make no sense of his words. She sat staring numbly, hardly aware of his remorseful expression. Then his meaning washed over her, and her skin seemed to shrink against the bones as color receded from her face.

"But why would he do that?" she finally managed to gasp.

Franklin shrugged uncomfortably. "I think the reason should be obvious. Through your efforts 'The Lady of Dordrect' was exposed as a forgery, and that embarrassed both Hamilton Corporation and the Hamilton family. Goodness knows, Paige, you should be commended for the job you've done, not fired. It took experience and expertise to detect the things wrong with that portrait, and you saved the museum from spending an enormous sum on a worthless acquisition."

Franklin sat down and took her icy hands in his. "You're one of the finest conservators I've ever known, better even than Evan was at your age. And as much as I hate to lose you as a member of my staff, I know Evan will hate it even more. He has great respect for your skill and judgment. I won't ever be able to make him understand the pressures that are compelling me to let you go."

"I'm not sure I understand them either." Paige gulped, still trying to comprehend what was happening. All that seemed to penetrate her chaotic thoughts was that Grant was behind what was happening, that, for some reason she couldn't fathom, he had turned against her. From the start she had been suspicious of his motives. A man as handsome, rich, and personable as Grant Hamilton had no business courting an ordinary woman like her, and she should have known better than to trust him. But everything had happened too fast. She had let him get too close, she had begun to care too much, and she had wanted so much to believe in him. But she couldn't think about Grant's betrayal now, not when there was even the slightest chance that she could change Arthur Franklin's mind.

"But I was right about the Hals!" she argued. "Doesn't that mean anything?"

Franklin sighed and stood up, resting his palms on the back of the chair. "Your dismissal really doesn't have much to do with being right or wrong about the portrait. You made two unforgivable mistakes: You cast Hamilton Corporation and the Hamilton family in a bad light, and you exposed a transaction they wanted to remain confidential. Your termination is retribution for those things."

"But that's not fair!" Paige burst out angrily. "Can't anyone reason with Mr. Hamilton?"

Franklin shook his head slowly. "It's obvious you don't know Hamilton very well, Paige, or you'd realize how futile that would be. He's an arrogant egomaniac who always gets his way, be it through threats, intimidation, or bribery."

Even after his inexplicable actions the previous night, Paige couldn't reconcile what she knew of Grant with Franklin's description of him, yet neither could she imagine him having her fired. He might be high-handed and overbearing, but she would never have characterized Grant as being malicious or vindictive. Was it possible she had misjudged the man so completely?

"Mr. Hamilton has threatened to cut off his company's funding to the museum if you don't do as you're told," Paige observed, thinking aloud.

The director nodded. "As always, Paige, you're very astute. Because his company is the museum's single largest contributor, I don't dare ignore Hamilton's wishes. I just can't afford to alienate him and his important friends. I've disagreed with his policies and his steamroller tactics before, but never more so than now."

When Paige made no reply, Franklin continued, "You

needn't leave the museum right away, Paige. Plan to stay at least until the end of next month, and we'll arrange a suitable severance pay to tide you over until something else comes along. You can count on me for a glowing recommendation, and I know Evan will feel the same way."

Paige took a deep breath. She was going to cry, and she didn't want to do it in front of Arthur Franklin. "I very much appreciate your concern," she managed to say in a choked voice, "and I understand your position perfectly. I wouldn't want to do anything to jeopardize the financial stability of the museum either. I'll be sure to let you know when I need one of those glowing recommendations." She had been speaking quickly and guiding him toward the exit, but he paused in the doorway.

"I want you to know how terribly sorry I am about this, Paige," the director reiterated.

She could hardly wait to send him away. "It's all right, Arthur," she babbled. "I don't hold you responsible for what's happened." How easy it was to absolve Arthur Franklin for his part in this travesty, she thought angrily, but there was another man who would never receive her forgiveness.

When Franklin was gone, she closed the door to the conservation lab, turned off the lights, and stumbled toward the table where "The Lady of Dordrect" lay. "This is all your fault!" she whispered. "All your fault!" Then with ragged, gulping sobs her tears came, in waves like wind-driven rain.

Instinctively she sought refuge in the high-backed wing chair in the window alcove and gave vent to her emotions. For a while she wept with single-minded grief, full of confusion and indignation. But as her tears subsided, she began to realize that even more devastating than the dismissal itself was the knowledge that Grant was behind it. Desperately she tried to find an excuse for his behavior, but even as she cast around for some kind of explanation, she knew there was none. Though he had threatened her position at the museum twice, she had never taken him seriously. She had foolishly imagined that being right about the Hals would offer her protection. The terrible injustice of what was happening infuriated her most.

How terribly wrong she must have been about Grant to have fancied herself in love with him. How naive and foolish she must have appeared to have allowed him access to her body and her heart while he was plotting betrayal. It was the ruthless egotist Arthur Franklin had described, not the man she knew, who had ordered her fired. But even so, she had forfeited dearly for misjudging Grant Hamilton's character.

Beneath her disillusionment and pain was a deep-seated anger directed partially at Grant but primarily at herself. She had suspected his ploy all along and had succumbed to his charms in spite of it. Now, because she had once again fallen victim to a good-looking man, she had jeopardized everything she had worked so hard to gain.

From the time she was twelve and had wandered into her first art history class at the small, exclusive women's college where her mother taught languages, Paige had known she wanted to work surrounded by great works of art. The thrill of appreciation that had crept over her in that stuffy, darkened lecture hall as images of Baroque and High Renaissance masterpieces had flashed on the screen had overwhelmed her. During the following years her enchantment had grown as she'd poured over the college's extensive slide collection and become familiar with the actual works themselves on frequent visits to museums in Boston and New York. At seventeen, she'd won a full scholarship to study art history at Princeton and had secured internships each summer at the National Gallery. That had led to postgraduate study at Winterthur and the Sorbonne and eventually a master's degree in conservation from the University of Delaware. She had pursued her goal single-mindedly except for her brief, ill-fated affair with Patrick Marshall during her junior year, which had nearly cost her the scholarship. Now, once again, her attraction to a handsome man threatened her dreams.

She had been a fool to get involved with Grant Hamilton, a fool to take him into her heart and into her bed when his intentions had been clear from the outset. Anger at her own folly burned even more brightly than her searing disappointment in him.

She stirred from her seat in the window alcove only long enough to make herself a pot of tea on the lab hot plate and call the switchboard with orders that she was not to be disturbed. Calmed by the passage of time and the soothing effect of her favorite herbal brew, Paige considered her options. She supposed she could fight the dismissal in the courts or through public opinion if she chose, but even as she considered the idea, she knew she would not. She could never do anything that could harm the people and the things she loved, and she knew she would not jeopardize the museum's reputation, or Grant Hamilton's either. She would go quietly when the time came, no matter what they had done to her.

It had been one hell of a day, Grant reflected as he returned to his office at Hamilton Corporation late that afternoon. His biweekly meeting with the development department this morning had been fruitful but time-consuming; then trouble with one of the machines on the main assembly line had gobbled up most of the afternoon. There were reports on his desk to be read, letters to be dictated, schematics on his drawing board that deserved his attention. But he was preoccupied by thoughts of his disastrous early-morning meeting with his brother.

Grant poured himself a cup of coffee from the pot on the credenza, grimaced at the bitter taste, and wandered to the window to stare out across Hamilton Industrial Complex and the airstrip beyond.

Anthony had been far more upset at the news that "The

Lady of Dordrect" was a forgery than Grant had ever anticipated. But even now he wasn't sure how much of his brother's response was linked to the financial ramifications of the discovery and how much was an outgrowth of his personal attachment to the painting. With Anthony it was hard to judge, but his response to what the museum had discovered had been thunderous.

"What do they mean, it's a forgery?" Anthony had shouted. "How the hell can that be? 'The Lady' has been shown all over the world as an example of Hals's best work. Why weren't her origins ever questioned before? The Tri-City Museum must be wrong!"

Then had come the words Grant had been anticipating since Friday afternoon. "How the hell could you let this happen?" Anthony had demanded furiously. "My God, Grant! I left you with a simple transaction to conclude, and you managed to screw it up!"

"Surely you realize none of this is my fault," Grant had defended himself. "But you can rest assured, Anthony, that however this turns out, I intend to take full responsibility for the situation."

"You're damned right you will," his brother agreed. "This is on your shoulders, Grant. If the museum brings charges of fraud against us, you're the one who will answer them. You can explain this fiasco to the board of directors, too. I just hope all this negative publicity doesn't jeopardize everything we've been working to prevent."

Grant had no need to be reminded of the ramifications or his own responsibility. "Believe me, Anthony, if anything I've done jeopardizes either Hamilton Corporation's reputation or its future, you'll have my immediate resignation."

As he'd turned to go, Grant had seen a cold gleam of satisfaction in his brother's dark eyes and felt a shudder of premonition deep inside.

Now, staring out across the runway, his grip tightened on the coffee cup as this morning's scene replayed in his mind. Why was the trouble with the company dividing he and Anthony when it should be uniting them? Did the problem go back to competitive feelings formed in their childhoods?

Seven years Grant's elder, Anthony had always been a perfect child, held up as someone to respect and emulate. Whether it was a function of the difference in their ages or his incompatibility with the role he was expected to play, Grant had never quite come up to the standards established by his older brother. Perhaps the early competition had led to the strained relationship between them now, to the bitter struggle being waged for control of Hamilton Corporation.

Even though Grant was an adult with self-confidence, insight, and considerable business acumen of his own, Anthony still had the power to evoke the insecurities of childhood to use against him. This morning those feelings had surfaced again, and Grant had questioned his own judgment in confronting the problem of the forgery.

But away from Anthony's inhibiting presence, his confidence returned. He felt compassion for his brother's disappointment, and he wished he could offer consolation and encouragement to Anthony. Still, the violent disagreement over the sale of the Hals and this morning's bitter words precluded any reconciliation between them.

Grant drained his coffee cup and sat down in the tall leather chair behind his desk. What seemed like a ream of phone messages littered his desk, and he flipped through the pile half-heartedly. In spite of his less than amicable parting from Paige the previous evening, he was mildly disappointed that none of the messages was from her. Needing a respite from the pressures of the day, Grant leaned back in his chair and punched the museum's number.

"Miss Paige Fenton, please," he said when the switchboard answered.

"I'm sorry, Miss Fenton isn't taking any more calls from the press," came the polite reply.

The response startled Grant. What kind of a day must Paige have been having? he wondered. Glancing down at the messages spread out on his blotter, he realized with a jolt of concern that more than half a dozen of them were from the news media.

"This is Grant Hamilton of Hamilton Corporation, not a reporter," he growled. "It's imperative that I speak to Miss Fenton immediately." Identifying himself for the operator's benefit worked the usual magic; she put the call through. By the seventh ring he was about to hang up when the line suddenly came alive.

"Hello?" Paige's voice sounded strained and muffled.

"Paige? This is Grant. What's the matter?"

There was a long, empty silence before she answered, and when she did, her voice quivered with what might have been anger or unshed tears. "How dare you call and ask me what's wrong? How dare you ask me anything after what you've done, you—you miserable, despicable lowlife!"

"Paige! What the hell's going on over there?" he demanded gruffly.

"Don't try to deny it, Grant Hamilton. I know you're behind this! I just wanted to believe that when I was proved right about the portrait you'd forget your threat." Her voice was definitely closer to tears than anger.

"Paige, calm down for a minute and explain what you're talking about," he began, adopting a reasonable tone with great effort. "What threat did I make?"

Paige drew an unsteady breath. "You said if I was wrong about the Hals, it would cost me my job. But I wasn't wrong. 'The Lady of Dordrect' is a forgery, and I've lost my job anyway. Arthur Franklin said I was fired on your orders, Mr. Hamilton."

Grant stared helplessly at the phone as his mind struggled to make sense out of her half-hysterical words. Instead he read volumes in all she hadn't said, and a terrible suspicion began to grow.

"Paige, please listen," he mumbled, but the line went dead before he had a chance to form his thoughts into any kind of coherent defense. He sat for a full minute with the lifeless phone cradled against his ear, then stabbed out the museum's number again and asked for the director's office. It was only when he was informed that Director Franklin was gone for the day that he realized how late it was getting. Hanging up the phone, he sat back and tried to decide what to do.

He considered seeking Anthony out, but Grant had neither the time nor the energy for another confrontation with his brother. Anyway, it was clear what had happened. Anthony had vented his anger on the person who had dared to proclaim the Hals a forgery. He had found out who made the accusations, then forced Arthur Franklin to fire Paige in retribution for having done her job too well.

A frown marred Grant's features as he toyed with the telephone cord. Finally he punched the museum's number a third time. Now that he had figured out what was going on, he had to talk to Paige and explain.

Instead of a human voice, a recording droned in his ear. "The Tri-City Art Museum is now closed. Regular museum hours are Tuesday through Saturday, ten A.M. to five P.M. Sunday from—"

"Dammit!" Grant mumbled under his breath, hung up, then quickly pushed the first digits of Paige's home phone. But before he was finished, he had reconsidered his actions. It would be infinitely easier to explain everything in person, he decided. Besides, Paige couldn't hang up on him if he was talking to her face to face. Ignoring the messages, charts, and reports that covered his desk, Grant snatched up his suitjacket and headed toward the parking lot.

Paige's apartment was empty when he let himself in, and he prowled around restlessly before taking a can of soda from the refrigerator and turning on the television set. The national news carried a story about the Hals forgery, with new footage as well as the videotape from the previous day's press conference. By the end of the broadcast Grant was jumpy and apprehensive. Still, there was nothing he could do about the publicity, and he knew he had to get things settled with Paige before he could devote himself to other matters. Surely she would be home soon. He helped himself to an apple and another soda.

By eight-thirty he'd had his fill of waiting and on impulse took her address book from the kitchen drawer and tried the museums's unlisted number.

"Tri-City Art Museum security office, Alan Fellows speaking."

"Mr. Fellows, this is Grant Hamilton," he began. "I have reason to believe that Paige Fenton is still in her office at the museum, and it's very important that I get in touch with her. Can you put this call through?"

The frigid silence at the other end of the line left little doubt that Fellows had heard about the circumstances of Paige's firing. "My system indicates that there is someone in that office, but the extension seems to have been left off the hook."

Grant gook a long breath. "Then I want you to let me into the museum so I can talk to Paige myself," he said as reasonably as he could.

"I'm sorry, Mr. Hamilton, I can't do that." Fellows's voice was carefully polite, but hostility crackled through the telephone wires like static. "It's against policy for anyone except museum personnel to be in the building after closing."

The man didn't seem the kind to respond favorably to blackmail, threats, or bribery, though Grant briefly considered all three. "Dammit, Fellows," he finally ground out in frustration, "I've got to talk to Paige!"

"It seems to me, Mr. Hamilton, that you've done quite enough talking to people at this museum. You ordered Director Franklin to fire her."

"No!" Grant denied. "My brother Anthony gave that order; I swear it. Only Paige doesn't know that. Please, Fellows, you've got to let me in to see her."

Fellows hesitated, obviously weighing Grant's argument.

Sensing the other man's conflict, Grant repeated his request. "Please, Fellows, let me into the museum. I promise I won't do anything to hurt Paige."

Perhaps it was the desperation in Grant's voice more than his words that convinced the security guard. "This is totally against policy," Fellows began, but Grant cut him short.

"I'll be at the service entrance in fifteen minutes!" he said. "And, Fellows, thank you."

CHAPTER
Eight

PAIGE STIRRED SLUGGISHLY in the large wing chair near the windows and set aside her teacup. She had watched the encroaching night swallow up the conservation lab, then creep to within a few feet of her chair, to be held at bay only by the illumination of a single lamp. During the quiet, tranquil time she had been able to empty her mind and dwell on nothing more complex than the never-ending cycle of daylight and dark. But as beneficial as these solitary hours had been, she knew it was time to leave her haven and return to the real world. There were no easy solutions to her problems with Grant Hamilton and the museum, but at least her time alone had given her perspective on them both.

The question of her job was by far the easier to resolve. Arthur Franklin had offered her good references, and she knew she could depend on Evan Rogers to stand behind her, too. If she could afford to wait until publicity over the Hals forgery died down, she might be able to slip in to a position in the conservation department of another museum.

Still, she knew her dismissal at such a crucial time and the undesirable publicity she had brought to the museum did not bode well for securing a comparable job. With a long breath she came to her feet, knowing full well that somehow she would make a place for herself in spite of everything.

It was only when she tried to plumb the depths of Grant Hamilton's motives that she was thwarted. Clearly he had used her, but to what end? Why had he pursued her when he knew he had nothing to gain? Why had he then turned ruthlessly against her and ordered her fired?

She moved to the worktable where the Hals portrait lay and switched on the overhead light. The woman who had lived and loved more than three centuries before mocked her. The serene smile was almost sneering, the cool gray eyes disdainful. Somehow Paige doubted that "The Lady of Dordrect" would have lost her heart to a man who meant only to discard her. She had a shimmering jade ring on her finger as a token of some man's desire, while all Paige had was a handful of memories. Perhaps things would seem brighter in the morning, she thought, placating herself with the platitude while she gathered her belongings and turned out the lights.

As she locked the door, the jangling of her keys seemed loud in the dark, silent corridor, and for no reason at all her palms went clammy. She had worked late often enough to know she was perfectly safe in the museum, yet her stomach tightened with uneasiness.

"Don't be foolish," she muttered and was surprised at how her voice echoed. Her skittish gait down the hall gave evidence of her apprehension, and for an instant it seemed as if she heard footsteps falling in counterpoint with her own. She stopped and stood motionless with her heart pounding high in her throat, hoping the almost tangible quiet in the museum would reassure her.

But the noises were not imaginary. The ringing of shoes on the stair treads was too fast and sure to belong to either of the elderly watchmen who patrolled the galleries. The only other possibility was that Alan Fellows had left the computer center to check on her. But the man who appeared silhouetted at the top of the stairway was both broader and taller than Alan. Any intruder in the museum at night clearly meant danger, and Paige sprinted toward the opposite stairway in terror. She thought the man might have called out to her as he followed, but with the sound of their feet pounding along the hall, Paige could not be sure.

At the second-floor landing she left the staircase and moved into the darkened galleries where her stealth and knowledge of the interconnecting rooms might offset his advantage of greater speed and strength. Sliding noiselessly along, her senses seemed to expand to amplify every particle of input, making her aware of every whisper of movement, every whiff of danger. She felt the intricate contours of the room with its pattern of display cases, saw every wink of light reflected on the shiny silver trays and tea sets within them, heard the monotonous whir of the complex climate-control system that kept the rooms at their optimum temperature and humidity.

Paige froze where she stood as the man paused in the doorway of the gallery in which she had taken refuge, and her body seemed to pulse with every beat of her heart as she awaited discovery. But finally he moved on, and she crossed into the rooms that housed the artifacts of primitive cultures.

Even in the light of day the art of the Pacific island people made her uncomfortable, but tonight, with her senses honed sharp, the sightless eyes and the gaping mouths of the Oceanic masks and fetish figures took on a new horror. In the darkness she seemed to be stalked not only by the lurking intruder but by the leering house posts and predatory bird-gods that hung from the rafters. She stole from one deeply shadowed alcove to another until she approached the stairs that led to the security office and safety.

Just then Paige caught a movement from the corner of her eye as a gush of air from the ceiling vent sent one of the suspended bird figures swaying. Involuntarily, she gave a soft, swiftly muffled cry of fear, and her pursuer loomed up in the doorway: huge, black, and utterly terrifying. She fled mindlessly back the way she had come.

Only her superior knowledge of the museum saved her as she dodged in and out of the maze of rooms that honeycombed the west end of the second floor. Finally she made her way to the opposite stairway and glided downward until she reached one corner of the huge main hall. From where she stood in one of the vaulted stone doorways, the passage to the new wing and the security office lay diagonally across the almost completely open space. Half a dozen sculptures were scattered at intervals along the polished marble floor, big pieces that were not dwarfed by the scale of the room. An information desk stood at the far end, but nothing offered her much in the way of protection. She might find sanctuary moving from sculpture to sculpture down the hall, she reasoned, but she would be vulnerable as she traversed the expanse between them. Still, she knew she had to try.

Taking a deep breath, Paige left the protection of the archway and raced toward the closest sculpture, a large, modern piece made of hollow-core steel panels that fanned out from the central point like the pages of an upended book, forming a series of sharp interior angles.

Just as she reached the shadowed safety between two of the rough steel sheets, the man she had been fleeing entered the cavernous room from the opposite end. In frozen fascination she watched as he moved toward her. There was something both familiar and predatory in the way he walked, but Paige could not think beyond her swelling panic.

He paused to search the information desk, then approached a gently swaying Calder mobile. Skirting it carefully, he checked both sides of the propellerlike blades that formed the base, then glided noiselessly toward a reclining bronze nude of monumental proportions. From the way he carried himself, she could tell he was extending each of his senses to compensate for what he couldn't see.

Then he came toward the massive abstract sculpture where Paige had taken refuge. She retreated deeper into the center of the piece, until she felt the gritty, untreated steel against her. If she were discovered, the sculpture would trap her helplessly.

Even before the man came into her field of vision, Paige knew he was there, as if his essence had already begun to intrude upon her. She waited, her heart tripping frantically, and then he stepped lightly around the hollow-core plate to her right and stood still. In the glow from the EXIT sign over the nearest door she could see the outline of his face and catch the glint of sun-streaked hair. Suddenly she went cold and tingly with recognition and moistened her lips to speak, but the sound was less than a whisper.

"Grant?"

His eyes narrowed as he probed the dimness. "Paige, is that you?" he asked, groping forward. "Paige, it was Anthony, not me, who had you fired."

He had known exactly what she had needed to hear, and every impulse within her demanded that she believe him.

"Anthony flew in from London this morning," Grant continued, "and without my knowledge or sanction called Arthur Franklin. This has been a terrible mix-up, but I'll make it right, Paige, I promise you!"

His actions more than what he said ultimately convinced her. Grant had come to the museum to find her, braving Alan Fellows to gain admittance, searching her out in the dark galleries to assure her of his concern. Waves of relief swept over her, relief at being safe, relief that Grant had not betrayed her, relief that things were not as black as they had seemed. She was overcome by a need to be held and soothed, a burgeoning desire to feel the hardness and strength of Grant's body against her.

She reached out to him. But with that touch it was as if a circuit had been closed and a jolt of current sliced through them both. Their senses had been honed by the chase through the deserted museum so that they came together in pure consciousness: overwhelmingly attuned, excruciatingly aware of each minute perception. Paige had no chance for refusal or denials, even if she had wanted to make them, as Grant dragged her into his arms.

The texture of his mouth excited her, the firmness of his lips and the moist darkness beyond. A gentle pull drew her deeper, and her tongue encountered the sensuous roughness of his. For a time she was lost in the wonder of him, the lingering fresh taste of the apple he'd eaten, the tangy scent of his skin. Her own inexplicable response turned her limbs to water.

His hands moved in ever-widening patterns across her back, as if claiming every inch of her for himself. Then he was tugging her blouse free of her waistband so his fingers could roam over her dewy flesh. Her muscles stretched and shifted against his palms as the firm, willowy strength of her came against him, and with evident impatience Grant stripped the buttons of her blouse from their holes and cast the garment aside. Paige shrugged out of her slip and bra, and his hands came up along her ribs to cup her full, pink-tipped breasts.

The tenderness of his touch was a promise fulfilled, and she arched her back as his lips claimed first one tightening nipple and then the other. Incandescent sensation licked through her, and at that moment she didn't know where she was, or who she was. She knew only that with this man, and this man alone, she might approach the brink of intangible ecstasy.

With a murmur of unintelligible words and a spate of burning kisses Grant bore her to the ground, and the rasp of rusting steel against her back was replaced by the ice-smooth chill of polished marble. In a single movement her stockings and underclothes were stripped away as Grant sought the haven between her thighs. His touch was potent, enflaming, and she urged him onward, craving unity as fiercely as he. Still in the midst of the tumult that engulfed them, he drew away, and when the first thrust came with a flare of fulfilling fire, she knew he had taken the ultimate responsibility for them both.

With that single stroke the last semblance of rational thought left them, and they felt nothing but the swift, surging needs of their bodies. Paige knew only the scalding heat of Grant above her, the sweet murmur of his breathless whispers, and the all-encompassing safety she found in his embrace. She saw nothing but the dark, shadowed face of the man who rode the whirlwind with her, and she watched as his pleasure and his need grew beyond all bearing.

Grant's arms tightened convulsively, holding her close as their world came apart, shattering around them until they were hurdling helplessly toward the total disillusion of self that is perfect rapture. Delight burst upon them, filling every level of their consciousness with more than their senses could hold. Yet even as they passed into the realm of pure pleasure, their gazes held, and for that flicker of eternity they were melded together, sharing total and complete communion.

How long they lay spent and sated beneath the sheltering planes of the abstract sculpture neither one could say. Awareness returned slowly, stealing in one sense at a time, unable to banish the dangerous languor that left them heavy lidded and immobile. Finally Grant stirred, rising above her on stiff arms while their bodies were still joined. His hair was in careless disarray; his shirt and suitjacket hung open, baring his chest, and his loosened tie hung comically askew.

"This is totally outrageous!" he exclaimed with a broad grin. It was obvious he was totally pleased with himself.

Paige looked up at him and realized that whatever had transpired in the past or whatever the future might bring, for this moment Grant Hamilton was hers. She intended to savor whatever time fate had given her.

"Do you mean the sculpture, Grant?" she asked, grinning impishly.

He stifled a chuckle and bent to kiss her. "You know damn well I don't mean the sculpture! Though I freely admit I've never much liked this artist's work, I think I'm developing a whole new appreciation for this particular piece."

A swift rejoinder bubbled to Paige's lips, but she bit it back as they became aware of voices and footsteps at the other end of the hall. Both Paige and Grant froze, knowing they would be completely compromised if they were discovered.

"Now remember, John," one of the voices warned as the night watchmen came nearer, "Alan says Miss Fenton and Mr. Hamilton are out here somewhere. Mind you don't stumble over them in the dark."

The comment was so close to the mark that both Paige and Grant dissolved into silent laughter as the second guard made an equally ribald reply. When the two men had moved on to patrol the galleries, Grant came to his feet, still chuckling to himself. His clothes were more or less where they belonged, but it took some groping in the dark to locate Paige's things. She stood shivering as he searched, and once she was fully dressed, she stared at Grant, waiting for him to speak. His disclosure that Anthony, not he, had had her fired answered only some of her questions.

Grant seemed to understand her confusion. He bent to kiss her by way of reassurance, then slung an arm around her waist as he led her toward the stairs. "I imagine Alan Fellows must be wondering what happened to me. I gave my word that I'd leave as soon as we got things settled, but I've been here all this time, and you and I haven't settled a damn thing."

"So it was Anthony and not you who called Arthur Franklin and had me fired," Paige reiterated as she dried the last

Portrait of a Lady

pan from the dinner of omelettes, toast, and salad she had thrown together when they'd returned to her apartment.

Grant let the water out of the sink and wiped the countertop with the dish cloth. "Exactly, but I'm going to get things straightened out with both of them first thing in the morning. If only I'd explained that Anthony was flying in from London today, you might have understood my behavior last night and at least a bit of what was going on this afternoon."

Paige set aside her towel and slipped an arm around his waist, nestling against him. After his abrupt withdrawal the previous evening and the confusion this afternoon, she needed to reestablish the closeness between them that came far more readily through physical channels than it did through intellectual ones. "It's all right, Grant," she murmured against his shirt front, "now that I understand everything."

A fleeting grimace touched the corners of his mouth, and his arm tightened, pulling her closer. "You don't know or understand everything yet, Paige, but after tonight you will." There was determination in his voice and a hint of something more that pleased Paige immeasurably.

"From now on, Paige, there will be no secrets between us." He bent to seal his promise with a kiss, reveling in the sweet swell of emotion that moved between them. This woman was very dear to him, far dearer than any woman had ever been. For that reason alone he felt compelled to share more and more of his life with her. After a moment he straightened, stripped the makeshift apron from the waistband of his trousers, and wiped his hands. "Let's go into the living room, all right?"

Paige preceded him, and Grant stopped to gather their wineglasses and the half-empty bottle of wine from the table.

"I think you need to understand why the sale of 'The Lady of Dordrect' was so important to me and to Hamilton Corporation, too," Grant began when they were comfortably seated on the white-slipcovered divan.

Paige settled into the corner of the couch, her eyes dark and intent.

Grant took a sip of wine, then set the glass aside. "As you know, Hamilton Corporation makes and sells all kinds of aircraft equipment—everything from the simplest artificial horizons to complex computerized systems for in-flight programs and navigation. Since before World War Two, about seventy-five percent of our business has been with the government, either directly or through primary aircraft manufacturers.

"About eighteen months ago, under my direct supervision, Hamilton Corporation bid on and won several very important government contracts. They were so big and so lucrative that they promised to double the company's worth. We'd made the deal of a lifetime, and everyone involved was ecstatic.

"After careful consideration, we decided we needed to expand our facilities to fulfill the new demand for our products. We had our architects draw up plans for new buildings on Hamilton Corporation's current site and for a subsidiary plant in Shale Valley. We bought land, hired a contractor, and began our expansion program.

"Everything was going along very well, and then without warning the entire project blew up in our faces. The government contracts were canceled, and we didn't know what to do. Every dime of the company's money was sunk into the construction, and we were committed to its completion, but without the government orders we would have no use for the buildings once they were finished. Then, too, we developed some cost overruns we'd never anticipated." His tone was deep and troubled as Paige's hand moved to cover his in a gesture of consolation.

"The financial picture was pretty grim," Grant continued. "We knew we couldn't solicit any more loans without running the risk of being gobbled up by one of those big conglomerates, and we wanted to avoid a takeover at all costs. So, for one of the few times in our lives, Anthony and I agreed on what we should do: We were going to use our own money to keep Hamilton Corporation afloat. But it wasn't as easy as we had hoped. Between the construction and the payrolls, it didn't take long to run through our liquid assets. In June we mortgaged the houses at Riverview and began to sell off the art collection."

"Then you lied at the press conference the other afternoon!" Paige exclaimed, surprised that he had taken her in so completely. "You lied when that reporter asked you why you were selling 'The Lady of Dordrect'!"

"Through my teeth!" Grant grinned. "I just hope everyone there was as credulous as you are, Paige."

Now that Grant was telling her the truth, she recalled clues to what the family had been doing that she hadn't previously understood. Sunday at the Hamilton estate she had seen no evidence of the legendary art collection that was reputed to be displayed there. She had been told that an exemplary piece of Maximillian armor stood in the front hall, but she hadn't noticed it. The fabulous twelfth-century madonna supposedly on display in the main parlor hadn't been there either. What else had they sacrificed to save Hamilton Corporation from bankruptcy? she wondered. The walls hadn't been stripped bare, but there had been no evidence that prodigious art collectors lived in the house.

Grant's house had had that same incomplete feeling, as if the furnishing was arrested and unfinished. Paige should have detected the odd discrepancies in both of the homes, but she had been too preoccupied with her conflicting feelings for Grant to notice much else.

"But if you've been selling off the art collection since June, why haven't I been aware of it?" she asked puzzled. "It's always noteworthy when work of the caliber of your family's collection comes onto the market; yet I haven't heard or read a thing."

Grant refilled their glasses and took another swallow of wine. "To avoid publicity, Anthony sold most of it privately to friends and acquaintances or through discreet dealers, rather than at public auction, even though the prices we get that way aren't as high," he explained. "If there's even a suspicion that we're selling the collection because Hamilton Corporation is in trouble, there could be a run on our stock that would ruin Anthony and me and put the company under. So in a way the press coverage we've received the last few days has been even more damaging than finding out that 'The Lady of Dordrect' is a forgery."

Paige nodded slowly, appalled to think that her actions might foil Grant's attempts to save the business that meant so much to him. "But if you're really in such dire financial straits that you're selling off your family's art collection, why are you shopping for limner portraits and driving a car worth tens of thousands of dollars?"

Grant sighed and pulled her toward him. Profoundly content just to hold her close, he rested his cheek against her fragrant hair before he continued. "It's all part of an elaborate masquerade," he told her. "Living as we've always lived rather than cutting back is a bluff in a high-stakes game we can't afford to lose. It's simply keeping up appearances. And besides, I do intend to buy the portrait of the little boy from Mr. Frasier when better times come."

"Will better times come, Grant?" she asked. "You and Anthony can't go on subsidizing Hamilton Corporation indefinitely."

The gentle brush of Grant's lips against her temple acknowledged her concern, and a smile tinged his voice when he answered her. "As a matter of fact, things are looking up. Many of the plans we made when we lost the government contracts are coming to fruition: My research people are about to announce a breakthrough that should give us an advantage over the rest of the industry, and Anthony has opened a new market by negotiating contracts with several aircraft manufacturers in England and on the Continent. If we can hang on through the first of the year, Hamilton Corporation should be out of the woods. But the money from the sale of 'The Lady of Dordrect' was supposed to buy us that time."

"What will you do now?" Paige wanted to know.

Pressed intimately against Grant, she felt him shrug. "I'm not really sure. Ride things out and hope for the best, I suppose. Anthony and I haven't really had a chance to discuss it."

Absently she toyed with a button on his shirt front. "I should think the problems at Hamilton Corporation would serve to bring you and Anthony closer," she observed in a low voice.

"I expected they would, too," he agreed, "but oddly enough they haven't. It's as if we both learned to be competitive and independent, but never mastered the arts of cooperation and compromise."

Something in his tone whenever he spoke of Anthony discouraged delving too deeply into his relationship with his brother; perhaps his reticence lay in the fact that he hadn't yet resolved the conflict himself. Smiling at her insight, Paige wisely changed the subject.

She raised her head and looked into his face, seeing not only the strong, handsome features but also the character and determination of the inner man. The fingers of her right hand moved to span the breadth of his jaw as her thumb traced the sensuously molded contours of his lips, and in his sapphire eyes she read a trust and vulnerability that touched her heart. He had shared his deepest secrets with her, things that no one else could know. He had proved his trust in her, secure that Paige would not betray him.

The fact that she loved him had never been more clear to her. She loved the texture of his face and hair, the passion in his touch, the husky timbre of his voice, and the fresh sun-washed scent of his skin. But even more she loved his sturdy grip on life's essentials, his innate understanding of what was important and what was not. He saw the value of openness and emotion, of honesty and caring, and she only wished she had recognized this facet of his personality in time to avoid the day's misunderstandings. Putting her trust in any man had always been difficult, Paige acknowledged, and from that realization came an apology as deep and sincere as her swiftly growing love.

"Oh, Grant, I'm so sorry about everything that's happened," she whispered. "I'm sorry about 'The Lady' being a forgery and that you might lose Hamilton Corporation because of it. I'm sorry about the publicity the discovery has brought. But most of all I'm sorry I doubted you. It was terribly unfair, and I should have known better."

That her words were heartfelt and sincere was evident, and as his mouth came down to claim hers, forgiveness and regret mingled freely. Her lips parted under the onslaught of his kiss, but Grant knew he dared not lose himself in her, at least not yet. There was so much more he needed to say, so much more he wanted to understand.

With a very real effort he raised his head to study her. She was beautiful in the lamplight—her face soft and her green eyes glowing with shimmering desire—but he fought the physical attraction, knowing there was more to her than an eager mouth and pliant body.

She really had believed he could betray her, and he needed to understand why. Choosing his words with care, he voiced the question that had lain between them from the very beginning: "Why don't you trust me, Paige?"

She shrugged out of his embrace and glanced away. "We didn't get off to a very good start," she offered lamely.

Grant reached across to take her hand, reestablishing the physical bond between them. "I think it's more than that," he coaxed. "Or do you mistrust all men?"

She reacted as if she'd been stung. "I don't mistrust men, I don't!"

Her vehement protest, as much as her shuttered expression, convinced Grant of the need to pursue the subject. "Don't you, Paige? I find that hard to believe when your actions belie your denials. Before you answer, just remember 'Secrets have the power to jeopardize all you hold dear.'"

As he turned the words of his fortune against her, Paige became aware of a threatening note in his voice and glanced up at him with a jolt of alarm. His confidences had reestablished the closeness between them, and she was loathe to do anything to destroy it. The answers to his questions were painful and difficult for her, but Grant was demanding no more of her than what he had already freely given.

She stared down at her tightly clasped hands as tears singed her eyelids. Of course she mistrusted men, especially men like Grant. He was everything her father had been: strong, vital, handsome. But hadn't Grant proved himself to her? He had allowed her to see behind his charming facade to the sensitive and vulnerable man inside. And because he had opened himself to her, didn't she owe him the truth?

Paige drew a long shuddering breath that seemed loud in the silence looming between them. "My—my father deserted my mother and me when I was four and a half," she stated baldly, appalled by how difficult that was to admit even now. "From what I can remember, he was a big, bluff man with hair the color of mine. Because he was a petroleum engineer, he traveled a lot, but when he came home, it was as if the sun had come out from behind a cloud. He always arrived with two or three of his friends in tow and with his pockets full of surprises. My mother would cook and clean for days before he was scheduled to arrive, and for a little while the house would be filled with piles of equipment, mysterious maps, and masculine laughter.

"Then I'd wake up one morning and they'd be gone, leaving Mother and me alone in an empty, silent house. Finally he simply stopped coming, and the house was empty and silent all the time. Oh, I'm sure there was more to it than that, but Mother never confided in me, not even when I was old enough to understand. It was a subject she refused to discuss.

"When I was seven we moved back East to an exclusive girls' school where Mother got a job teaching languages. Living in a little house on campus, I never did meet many other men. Mother seemed to enjoy the academic life and was content in her friendships with other women. In time I got caught up in that life, too."

Paige's voice faded into silence, and she was very aware that Grant was watching her thoughtfully. "And I suppose that once you left that cloistered environment, you met some egotistical bastard who reinforced your doubts about men in general."

Something in Grant's voice was both outraged and protective, and it gave her the courage to slowly nod her head. Paige was unwilling to discuss her college infatuation with Patrick Marshall, and Grant didn't need to know how much of a fool she'd been. She'd given Patrick her heart, her body, and her time researching his doctoral thesis, while she let her own work slide. For her effort, for all her hours of rewriting and typing Patrick's papers, for all the weeks of catering to his needs and nurturing his ego, she had received nothing but a cool kiss and a quick good-bye before he'd abandoned her to accept a teaching position at Stanford. Gorgeous, red-haired Patrick had used her just as her handsome, virile father had used her mother. So if Paige mistrusted men, it was because she had just cause.

Grant had been sitting quietly, content to hold her hand while she battled with her demons, but when it became evident that she had no more to say, he brushed her cheek with gentle fingers and turned her face to his. "It might be wise," he observed softly, "to try to keep your feelings for your father and whatever other bastards you've come across from tempering your relationships with other men."

She acknowledged the wisdom of his words with another nod of her head, wishing it were easier to do as he'd suggested. But behavior patterns were ingrained, and it would take time and effort to change them. Was Grant willing to be patient with her? she wondered. Did he care enough to help her find her way?

The quiet in the apartment was deep and mellow as they sat holding hands. Paige could hear the trees outside her open windows whispering in the wind and feel the cool, astringent breeze stroke along her skin. The air smelled as spicy and crisp as a tree-ripened apple, and she welcomed the promise of the approaching fall.

"It's getting late," Grant remarked, cocking his head to listen to the rhythmic cadence of the antique schoolhouse clock hanging in the dining alcove.

"Yes, it is," Paige agreed and moved a little closer as she lost herself in the brilliant warmth of his blue eyes. Without volition her free hand came up to caress his cheek as she slanted her mouth across his, tracing its inner contours with her tongue. "Are you going to spend the night?"

His lips quirked up at the right corner, and Paige felt, rather than saw, his teasing smile. "I've been drinking your wine all evening, so I really shouldn't drive home."

Paige withdrew and gave him a hard look. "Is that the only reason you're staying?" she demanded with mock severity.

His smile became a grin before he pulled her close and kissed her. "You must learn to trust me, Paige," he chided her at last. "I'm going to stay because, as close as I came to losing you today, I need to hold you, just hold you close for a very long time."

His words brought a flush of pleasure to her cheeks and gave her the courage to tease him, too. "And is that all you're going to do, just hold me?"

Grant's smile deepened, crinkling the corners of his eyes. "We'll start with holding and see where it goes from there."

"Then turn out the light, Grant," she invited. "I think it's time for bed."

He reached for the switch on the wall behind the couch, and a moment later the apartment was plunged into warm, intimate darkness.

CHAPTER
Nine

GRANT SANK LOWER in the high-backed chair, stretched his jean-clad legs before him, and waited for Anthony to finish preparing his drink. It was odd to be invited to Riverview's main house, and odder still to be treated as a guest. Ever since he had received Anthony's summons this afternoon, Grant had been profoundly curious. What did his brother want to discuss? And how long would it take before Grant could get back to his own agenda? An emergency at the Shale Valley construction site had kept him from approaching Anthony earlier on the question of Paige Fenton's dismissal, but before he left tonight, Grant meant to have the matter settled between them.

A tender smile touched his lips as he envisioned the way Paige had looked that morning: vague and sloe-eyed with sleep, her face pale and soft in the dawn light. She was a fascinating woman: complex, contradictory, unpredictable, but warm and giving beyond his wildest dreams. He longed to resolve the matter with Anthony quickly and discharge his promise to have Paige reinstated at the museum so he could escape from the day's difficulties in her arms.

Abruptly Grant became aware that Anthony was standing over him, offering him a tumbler of whiskey and water. Grant accepted it, took a sip, and set the glass aside. "Now, just why did you want to see me?" he asked.

The other man settled in the chair beside Grant's and savored the liquor before he replied. "I've read the reports from the art museum over and over, and though I've really tried to believe them, I'm not convinced 'The Lady of Dordrect' is a fake. There are just too many unanswered questions for me to accept the findings." Anthony waved Grant to silence when he would have interrupted. "Don't you wonder how a painting with so much history and provenance can turn out to be a forgery? And how was it that a Hals expert like Phillip Argenta was fooled?"

Grant shook his head. "Those aren't new questions, Anthony. I asked them at the museum myself, but I can't believe that chemical and microscopic tests lie."

Grant saw a flare of anger in his brother's dark eyes, but when Anthony spoke his voice was cool. "Nevertheless, I finally managed to locate Mr. Argenta, and on the strength of his recommendation, I have an appointment tomorrow to have 'The Lady of Dordrect' evaluated by the Chicago Art Institute."

Grant wasn't surprised at his brother's temerity; Anthony never gave in to anything without a fight. "And just what do you hope to prove?"

Anthony's fingers clenched around the crystal tumbler. "I hope to prove 'The Lady of Dordrect' is genuine. Isn't that what you want, too?"

Grant's thoughts turned to Paige. She had been so passionately sure about the portrait. Could she have been mistaken? What effect would further tests have on her position?

"The portrait we've hung in a place of honor all these years," Anthony continued, "the portrait Mother loved, is either genuine or such a good fake that even the experts were fooled. Don't you want to know which?"

"Lies, no matter how well told, remain lies," Grant pointed out softly. "Has Arthur Franklin agreed to let you take the portrait to Chicago?"

"Of course he's agreed," Anthony said angrily. "What choice does he have? To refuse further examinations implies their tests are in error. He believes their results will be verified, but I know differently."

Anthony's face glowed with a fervent zeal that made Grant inexplicably uneasy.

"And it's because the painting is scheduled for evaluation tomorrow morning," Anthony went on, "that I needed to talk to you tonight."

"Why? What does that have to do with me?"

"The agreement I made with Franklin was that one of us and someone from the Tri-City staff would take the painting to Chicago and return tomorrow night with the Art Institute's report."

"And who has Director Franklin decided to send?" Grant asked, already sensing the answer.

"He's sending the woman who started all this trouble, their associate conservator, Paige Fenton."

Grant saw disaster barreling down on him like a runaway freight train, and did his best to get off the tracks. "Well, don't expect me to go with her. I'm not getting any more mixed up in the question of the painting's authenticity than I already am."

"Dammit, Grant. As much as I'd like to see that bitch put in her place, I can't go. Will Meyer and an executive from Fokker are flying in from Brussels tomorrow to sign some contracts. That means this duty falls to you."

Grant shook his head in silent refusal. "Paige believes the painting is a forgery, and the tests so far have totally confirmed her allegations. Surely the Art Institute will only

Portrait of a Lady 127

echo Tri-City's results. Why can't you simply accept what's already proven? Besides, I should think you'd want to avoid the chance that news of your actions might leak to the press."

"God knows there's been too much publicity over this mess already," Anthony conceded, "but I don't understand why you aren't willing to question the results of the tests. Phillip Argenta swears they're wrong. He swears 'The Lady of Dordrect' really is a Hals. And I'm more than willing to believe him. Why aren't you? Don't you care about the future of Hamilton Corporation?" Almost as an afterthought he added, "And how long have you been on a first-name basis with our nemesis at the museum?"

Grant squared his broad shoulders and faced his intimidating elder brother. He'd intended to broach the subject of Paige's dismissal without alluding to his relationship with her, but he'd unintentionally revealed himself. "I've spent quite a bit of time with Paige Fenton during the past few days. She's an uncommonly bright and competent woman, and I'd accept her assessment of the painting now, even if the tests hadn't proved her correct. She's an expert in her field, and in spite of the unanswered questions and Phillip Argenta's protests, I trust her judgment implicitly."

Anthony seemed to weigh his brother's response before he spoke. "And yet, in spite of her intelligence, competence, and good judgment, Arthur Franklin has dismissed her from her position at the museum. Did you know that?"

Anger flushed Grant's cheeks, and his blue eyes narrowed. "He fired her on your orders, Anthony," he raged. "On your orders!" How clearly Grant remembered the expression of betrayal on Paige's face the night before when she'd thought him guilty of the deed. "Nor do I intend to stand idly by and condone such a gross injustice. Paige deserves to be commended for her discovery, not dismissed because of it. You won't get away with this, Anthony; I'll see that you don't. Paige is a fine conservator, and I won't allow her career to be sacrificed—"

Anthony drew a sudden deep breath. "You're in love

with Paige Fenton, aren't you?" he accused.

Grant paused in his tirade, astounded by Anthony's observation. It was an idea he hadn't yet put into words, but it had been hovering at the edge of his consciousness, awaiting definition and expression. "Yes, I am," he freely admitted after a moment. "I am in love with Paige Fenton, but my feelings have nothing to do with my insistence that you right the wrong you've done her!"

The room fell silent as both brothers became busy with their own thoughts. Grant's circled wildly between joy and astonishment. He had indeed fallen in love with Paige—swiftly, completely, and without volition. He had no doubts about his feelings. He was in love with her—with her wit, intelligence, and competence, with her beauty, vulnerability, and understated charm. Somehow she answered a need in him, a need to be protective and caring, a need to be open and trusting. The wonder of it took his breath away. Then a jolt of uncertainty zigzagged along his nerves. Was it possible that Paige didn't feel the same way?

Suddenly and desperately he wanted to have her warm and soft beside him, to hold her close and yielding in his arms. He longed to feel her hands and lips on his body, and ached to find reassurance in her embrace.

He became slowly aware that Anthony was standing over him, his empty glass in hand. "Can I get you another drink, Grant?" he asked softly, indicating the one that stood untouched on the table. Without thinking, Grant drained the contents of the glass and offered it to his brother.

In the few minutes it took Anthony to fulfill his duties as host, Grant had time to readjust his thinking in the light of this new realization. Fiery determination swelled through him to strengthen his resolve. No one was going to treat the woman he loved the way Anthony had treated Paige, he decided. No one, not even his brother. When Anthony returned with their freshened drinks, Grant was totally prepared to confront him.

"I want Paige Fenton reinstated as associate conservator at the Tri-City Museum first thing tomorrow morning," Grant announced without preamble as the other man resumed his seat. "And I'd like you to call Director Franklin personally. The wording of the apology you'll make to Paige is, of course, up to you. But I want it offered and accepted by Friday evening so that there won't be any unpleasantness if we should meet you at the opening of the Northern Light exhibit."

Grant was like a victor dictating terms of surrender, but Anthony met those demands with a proposition of his own. "If you agree to take 'The Lady of Dordrect' to the Art Institute tomorrow for reevaluation, and the experts concur with Tri-City's findings, as you're sure they will, I'll have a reason to call Franklin and have Paige Fenton reinstated. It will give me a chance to save face, Grant. Otherwise I'll look like a fool."

Grant understood his brother's reluctance to admit he'd been wrong. It wasn't an easy thing for any man to do, and the Hamilton pride was a hard master. He was implacably determined that his brother would offer Paige a sincere apology, but what harm could it do to let Anthony maintain his status with a man like Arthur Franklin?

"And if the Art Institute doesn't concur?" Grant pressed him. In spite of his empathy, he knew his brother too well to leave anything to chance. "What will happen if the Art Institute's experts don't agree?"

"Are you admitting that there is some doubt about the validity of Tri-City's findings?" Anthony countered. "Do you think your lady love is wrong?"

"I have complete trust in Paige's judgment," Grant assured him. "I just want this settled between us."

"Well, then," Anthony went on with a show of bravado, "I suppose you might be willing to wager Miss Fenton's position against the outcome of the Art Institute's reports, just to make things interesting. If she should be proven wrong, and 'The Lady of Dordrect' is indeed a genuine example of Hals's work, her dismissal from Tri-City Museum stands."

Grant was feeling vaguely confused by his brother's words and wondered how Anthony had managed to turn the tables on him. A few minutes ago he had been the one dictating terms, with Anthony begging for concessions. Now that situation was suddenly and inexplicably reversed.

A reckless need inside him rose to meet his brother's challenge, the same deep-seated competitive response to Anthony's goading that had haunted him all his life. Yet he was hesitant to gamble with Paige's future. There must be more to this arrangement than he could see, Grant reasoned slowly, suspicious of his brother's motives. Anthony seldom took risks without a chance to profit. Grant knew there must be a contingency beyond his grasp, but somehow it eluded him.

"I thought you believed in Paige Fenton's allegations," Anthony nettled him. "You said you had implicit faith in her judgment."

"I do!" Grant snapped, provoked by his brother's tone. "And to prove my trust in Paige's opinions, I accept your wager."

The gleam of triumph that shone in his brother's dark eyes made Grant profoundly uneasy, but before he could soften or call back the words, Anthony was redefining the conditions.

"If the Art Institute's report concurs with Tri-City's, then your lady will be reinstated with my apologies," he reiterated. "But if Paige Fenton is proven wrong, she's out of her job at the museum."

Apprehension filled Grant, but he knew he'd already agreed. Slowly he nodded.

"Then, to the Art Institute's report," Anthony toasted, raising his glass to his lips.

"And to Paige Fenton's vindication," Grant returned, before drinking from his own.

Portrait of a Lady

After the toast, Anthony settled back in his chair and began to review the arrangements he'd made for the trip to Chicago. As he spoke, Grant found it increasingly difficult to concentrate on his brother's instructions. His thoughts became random and diffused, wandering to things that had no bearing on tomorrow's activities: the vibrant, shifting patterns in the Oriental carpet, the droning tone of his brother's voice, the overwhelming warmth of the room. He forced himself to sit up straighter in the chair and listen to the flow of words, which suddenly, sounded slurred and distant on his ears. He struggled with the urge to let his eyelids close as a slow, debilitating wave of dizziness washed over him.

"I think . . . I think the drink you gave me went right to my head," Grant murmured groggily as a second, even more devastating wave of dizziness swirled around him.

Anthony's face seemed to float above him, and his brother's voice was filled with concern. "You don't look well, Grant. Would you like to lie down?"

Grant stirred clumsily in the chair and shook his head. "No, I need to call Paige and tell her what's happened," he insisted stubbornly. With steely determination he hauled himself to his feet, accepting Anthony's arm to steady him until the room stopped spinning. "Never been so drunk on so little liquor," he mumbled almost incoherently.

"You must be exhausted from all that's gone on these past weeks, to have a single Scotch affect you so," Anthony commiserated. "Why don't you call her from your old room, then lie down and spend the night."

Acknowledging the suggestion with a nod, Grant wavered toward the door.

"Call Paige, call Paige, call Paige," he whispered to himself as he fought his way up the stairs, drawing strength from the repetitious rhythm of the litany.

Once in his old room, Grant sat on the edge of the bed and hunted for the first digits of her number on the phone. But the buttons kept going in and out of focus, making dialing impossible. Then, with a low moan of defeat, Grant fell backward on the bed as the room spun around him, fading inexorably to black. He lay limp and immobile for a very long time, the telephone receiver still cradled against his ear.

CHAPTER
Ten

GRANT CLOSED HIS eyes against the dizzying blur of greenery and buildings that swept past the limousine window. Never in his life had he awakened with a hangover as virulent as this one. Surely the drinks he'd had last night with Anthony couldn't be responsible for his persistent queasiness or the fierce headache that beat inside his skull, but there was no other explanation for the way he felt.

As the car pulled up at the rear door of the Tri-City Museum, he put aside thoughts of his discomfort and focused on the woman emerging from the building. In spite of the promise he had made to Paige, he hadn't really resolved the question of her dismissal, and he was loath to explain the agreement he'd made with Anthony concerning it. Even though he had no doubt about what the tests would prove, he wasn't anxious to tell Paige that her tenure at the museum was dependent on the Art Institute's findings.

Once she had surrendered the carefully wrapped parcel that contained "The Lady of Dordrect" to the chauffeur for storage in the trunk, Paige climbed into the back seat of the limousine beside Grant. Dressed in a pale-lilac linen suit and creamy cut-work blouse that bared a long expanse of silky throat, she was exquisite. But with her red-brown hair knotted at the nape of her neck and her huge tortoise-shell glasses guarding her expression, she also seemed aloof and businesslike.

"Good morning," Grant greeted her.

"Good morning, Grant," she returned softly.

Sensing uncertainty in her tone, he hurried to reassure her. "I'm sorry I missed calling you last night, but I was at Shale Valley all day and didn't have a chance to talk to Anthony until rather late."

"I'd begun to wonder what happened," she admitted. "But you did get things resolved with him, didn't you?"

As the car began to move, Grant swallowed around the clot of nausea that rose in his throat. "Actually, it didn't turn out quite as I'd hoped," he confessed reluctantly.

Paige sat up a little straighter. "Oh?"

This wasn't the way he wanted to explain to her about his bargain with Anthony, a bargain he wasn't at all happy he had made. But there was little to be gained by waiting. "I want you to understand, Paige, that it was Anthony's idea to have the Art Institute reevaluate 'The Lady of Dordrect,' not mine," he began. "And on the strength of Phillip Argenta's recommendation, Arthur Franklin could not refuse."

"Yes, I realize that, but what does their evaluation have to do with my position at the museum?"

"It has a great deal to do with it, I'm afraid." Grant took a long breath, wishing he had never talked to his brother about Paige's job. If he had approached Franklin directly, he would never have been drawn into this ridiculous agreement, and Paige's position would be safe no matter what happened. "Anthony has agreed that if the Art Institute confirms your allegations about 'The Lady of Dordrect,' you will be reinstated."

His tentative tone had a ring of deception, and Paige was instantly suspicious. "And if the Art Institute's experts don't agree?" she pressed him.

Grant hesitated, trying to think of a way to temper the truth. "If they disagree with your findings, the dismissal from the Tri-City Museum stands. But, Paige," he hurried on, sensing her uneasiness, "we both know what those tests will prove. 'The Lady' is a forgery. I wouldn't have agreed to Anthony's conditions if there was any doubt in my mind about the portrait's authenticity."

There was a quick intelligence and an accusation of betrayal in her eyes as she faced him. "You promised me something, Grant," she began. "Something I'm entitled to, something I've earned. You promised that my position at the museum was secure, and now you tell me there are conditions on that promise. If I understand you correctly, my future is going to be decided by coldblooded outsiders, outsiders who have no idea what's at stake!"

He shook his head in silent negation, but she continued, her growing anger more than obvious. "I'm not a pawn in your corporate chess game, Grant. Nor will I let you barter my career in some convoluted sibling rivalry that will never be resolved."

His hand rose in a gesture of entreaty. "Paige, please, it's not like that at all! If only you'll let me explain—"

"I don't expect explanations from you, Grant," she told him frigidly. "Or reprieves, either. So let's not have any more excuses or promises between us, shall we?"

She turned away as if he weren't there, and before he could think of anything to refute her charges, they were pulling up at the Hamilton Corporation air field, where the company jet was waiting for them.

The rough flight and the effort it took Grant to control his unaccustomed air sickness precluded any further conversation betwen them. But by the time they had turned "The Lady of Dordrect" over to Richard Robusto, the curator of European painting at the Art Institute, and were standing before the museum's impressive facade, Grant felt better and was beginning to enjoy the prospect of spending the day with Paige. In spite of their argument, the situation seemed rife with possibilities.

"Well, how shall we spend our time in Chicago?" he asked, determined to use the day to best advantage. "We could play tourist and see the sights, visit the art galleries and antique shops, or catch a matinee. I think the Cubs are in town, if baseball interests you, or we could walk up to Water Tower Place and shop."

Paige turned to him coldly, angry and unforgiving. "Frankly, Grant, I don't give a damn what you do. I've made plans of my own. So if you'll excuse me—" She stepped to the curb and waved a hand. "Taxi!"

Grant came up behind her and caught her arm, whirling her around. "Now, just a minute, Paige. You're not going anywhere until we've had a chance to talk."

"Oh, really?" she snapped as she struggled against his grip. "After our conversation in the limo this morning, I don't think I want to hear anything else you have to say!"

"For godsake, listen to me, Paige," he hissed. "Can't you trust me at least a little?"

"Trust you? Why should I?" she demanded, succeeding in twisting free of his grasp. "Taxi!"

A bright-yellow cab swerved across two lanes of traffic and pulled up beside her. "Is that guy bothering you, lady?" the driver growled as she dove into the back seat.

"No! Oh, please, just get me out of here!" Paige gasped. As they lurched off into the melée with a clamor of horns, she could see Grant sprinting after them, dodging past vendors and pedestrians on the sidewalk until the cab outdistanced him.

"You okay now, honey?" the driver asked almost paternally when they had traveled a few blocks north on Michigan

Avenue. He was a big, brawny man, and Paige appreciated his concern. "Would you like me to take you home?"

"I want to go to the Field Museum, please," she replied, trying to convince both him and herself that the museum was indeed where she wanted to go.

Finding herself in the echoing main hall a few minutes later, Paige ducked between two of the mammoth columns and into the galleries that housed the American Indian exhibits. She had read about a new installation of artifacts from the Eskimo and Northwest Coast tribes and intended to spend at least part of her day there.

As she wandered through the display of dioramas and artwork, one part of her mind admired the skillful exhibit design and impressive display of chilkat blankets and dugouts, while another dwelt on this morning's disclosures. She was devastated that Grant could have callously bartered her future in his ongoing power struggle with his brother, and it hurt to know how little she meant to him. He had blithely abandoned the promise he had made her, and gambled with her position as well.

Yet she didn't doubt her allegations about "The Lady of Dordrect." What made her apprehensive was that she knew how inexact a science forgery detection could be. Controversy over the authenticity of pieces in museums all over the world raged as fiercely as any medieval battle. And Paige was justly worried about her own situation. Grant's agreement with his brother put her in a completely untenable position, and she was terrified of being manipulated for someone else's gain.

Finding a bench in the last gallery of Indian art, Paige settled back to inspect the collection of totem poles arrayed before her. But even as she studied the vivid carvings with their bright paint and mystic symbolism, she couldn't put Grant out of her mind.

She hadn't lost faith in his promise when yesterday had passed with no word. Not even when Arthur Franklin had come by to tell her about the tests at the Chicago museum.

She'd felt an odd uneasiness as the evening wore on without hearing from Grant, but she'd gone to bed with the staunch belief that everything would turn out as he had promised. Only this morning had she discovered that her position at the museum was as tenuous as before.

In spite of the importance of the Art Institute's report, it was Grant's apparent duplicity in fulfilling his promise that distressed her most. In a very short time Paige had come to care deeply for him, but clearly he didn't reciprocate her feelings. She couldn't mean much to Grant if he behaved as he had. Knowing that she was nothing more than a pawn in the dangerous game he and his brother had played all their lives hurt far more than anything else. The realization brought tears to her eyes, and she brushed them away, drawing the remnants of her pride close to comfort her.

Once, Grant had angrily accused her of feeling secure only in a museum's cloistered surroundings. Perhaps it was true. She had come to the Field Museum seeking the sanctuary of its solitude and anonymity. Its halls were spacious and quiet, its visitors dispersed and impersonal, its displays inanimate and undemanding. It was the perfect place to renew herself before she faced whatever the afternoon might bring. Slowly she stood up and moved toward the next bank of big glass cases.

Grant watched in frustration as the yellow taxi disappeared up Michigan Avenue, a bevy of its brothers closing ranks behind it to make further pursuit impossible. Paige was lost to him now, at least temporarily, and he frowned, thinking he had spent far too much time this past week dealing with the same frustrations—not knowing where Paige was, needing desperately to explain away some obstacle that had loomed up between them.

He loved Paige; loved the warm, protective way she made him feel about her; loved the confidence and strength she made him feel within himself. But since he did love her, why was it so hard to maintain the trust in their relationship?

They hadn't met under the best circumstances, he'd admit that, and Paige did have her own reasons for mistrusting men. But once they had overcome their initial animosity, they had opened themselves to share a deep, exquisite passion and a wealth of understanding. The fact that Grant's senses sang every time he touched her, that his most profound contentment came when Paige was by his side, made it imperative that they resolve their differences. He loved her, and he had to find a way to make things right between them.

The declaration of his love was the last totally clear memory he had of the previous evening. He could remember Anthony's appalled accusation and his own admission of his feelings. That the revelations had come so suddenly, so easily, so completely free of regrets, stunned him. Never in his life had he been so sure of his own emotions or so uncertain of their reciprocity. Was Paige's anger this morning caused by the position he'd forced on her, or in response to her insecurity about his feelings for her? How desperately he wanted to find and reassure her that however the Art Institute's tests came out, they would face the results together.

Grant started up the street, feeling the crisp breeze from the lake on his skin, seeing the resoundingly blue sky echoed in the city's glass buildings. It promised to be a fine day, and since it seemed futile to try to locate Paige in a city this size, he decided to go to a Cubs game.

But by noon, when he was ready to catch a cab for Wrigley Field, the weather had turned, and the air was heavy with an approaching storm. Wisely Grant ducked into a men's shop and bought an umbrella. Before the game was over, the rain arrived, sending unprepared fans racing for cover.

As he headed back to the Art Institute shortly after three,

comfortable and dry in the taxi, he hoped that wherever Paige was, she'd had enough presence of mind to buy herself an umbrella.

When Paige emerged from her virtual hibernation in the Field Museum a few minutes before four, the pelting rain that pummeled the streets and sidewalks surprised her. A no-holds-barred midwestern thunderstorm was deluging the city. It had already filled the storm drains and turned the sky a twilight purple. From the protection of the pediment that capped the museum's massive columns she could see Lake Michigan boiling up over the concrete breakwater and battering the boats in the small marina.

Unpleasant though the weather was, she had no choice but to venture out in it and hail a cab to take her to the Art Institute.

Even before she reached the bottom of the broad stairs that led to the street, she was soaked to the skin by the huge spattering drops. After a full ten minutes of waving frantically at the few cabs that passed, she accepted the hopelessness of the situation. She was at least moderately familiar with the part of Chicago that lay between the Field Museum and the Art Institute, and since she couldn't catch a cab, she decided to walk.

Lowering her head against the rain, she darted toward the nearest pedestrian bridge that led across the railroad yards to the string of hotels lining the west side of Michigan Avenue. Once on the narrow span, she felt the full force of the wind-driven rain for the first time. It came in howling waves of wetness that dashed against her with stunning impact, accompanied by incandescent flashes of lightning and roaring thunder that seemed to make the bridge shudder beneath her feet. It molded her soaking clothes to her and tore the pins from her heavy, streaming hair, leaving it clinging to her face and shoulders.

Paige was gasping for breath when she reached the Michigan Avenue end of the bridge, more from the exertion of fighting her way against the wind than from an attempt to hurry.

Once she crossed the street, the wall of buildings protecting her from the wind made walking easier, though no drier. The rain still fell in a hissing deluge, and cold seeped through her, sending chills down her spine. As she continued up Michigan Avenue, she paused briefly to check the time on an ornate clock in a jeweler's window. She was already half an hour late for her appointment.

She ran the last few blocks to the museum, and arrived there at four forty-five, breathless, trembling from the cold, and dripping. When she appeared in the doorway of Richard Robusto's office, Grant sprang to his feet.

"We were growing quite concerned over your whereabouts, Miss Fenton," the curator greeted her. "Mr. Hamilton was fully prepared to call the police if you didn't turn up in the next few minutes."

Paige sent Grant a curious glance, but his expression was impossible to fathom. "There was no reason to worry. I just couldn't find a cab."

"Well, whatever the reason, I'm glad you've arrived safe and sound. Now, won't you come in and have a seat while I go over the museum's findings?"

"Yes, Paige, come in and sit down," Grant said, pulling out the chair beside his own. "I think you'll want to be sitting down when you hear Mr. Robusto's news."

Paige sank gratefully into the chair, her knees gone suddenly weak. "Do you mean you found 'The Lady of Dordrect' is genuine, Mr. Robusto?"

"That's precisely what we found, my dear. As a matter of fact, it's as fine a Hals as I've ever seen."

Paige stared at the curator open-mouthed. "But how can that be when Tri-City's tests proved beyond the shadow of a doubt that 'The Lady of Dordrect' is a forgery?"

"I can't answer for the procedures your conservator used, but our examination of the portrait was very thorough. The painting you brought us this morning is unquestionably genuine and unequivocably Fran Hals's work."

Paige was speechless, both because of Robusto's findings and because of the devastating effect those findings would have on her life.

When it became clear she was incapable of further comment, Robusto continued. "By way of explanation, Miss Fenton, I suggest you read over the report I gave Mr. Hamilton. It outlines our procedures and the results of the tests we ran. I think once you've looked it over, you will be as convinced as we are that the painting is a genuine Hals. Now, since the museum is closing, I'm afraid I must ask you to go."

Grant expressed his thanks and shook hands with Robusto before tucking the carefully wrapped portrait under one arm and Paige's arm under the other. As he headed for the Michigan Avenue exit, Paige walked numbly beside him, aware only of her confusion and despair. She had been totally wrong about the portrait, completely and utterly mistaken about its authenticity. But how could that be when she had been so confident, so sure? And now that her world was crumbling in ruins around her, what was she going to do? What on earth was she going to do?

Along with the rest of the Art Institute's visitors, they were shepherded out the museum's main doors onto the busy, rain-washed street. Taking refuge from the weather with a throng of other people huddled beneath the arches of the open portico, Grant deliberately nudged Paige closer to the back wall so that when he spoke both his body and the portrait blocked any route of escape.

"Our flight home has been cancelled because of the weather, so I'm taking you to the company apartment to dry off and spend the night," he informed her matter-of-factly.

Paige slowly raised wide, accusing eyes to him. The last thing she wanted was to contend with Grant Hamilton and his victory. "I'm not going anywhere with you, Grant, least of all to the company apartment. I've found it unwise to

Portrait of a Lady

fraternize with my enemies, and I'll be damned if I'm going to spend another night alone with you."

He muttered something vulgar under his breath and loomed closer. "You'll do as I tell you, Paige, or I'll take you to the apartment by force! I don't intend to spend another minute wondering where the hell you are and if you're safe. You and 'The Lady of Dordrect' are my responsibility, and I'm not going to let either one of you out of my sight until we get to the Tri-City Museum tomorrow."

Stretching up to her own impressive height, she glared back. "I can understand your concern for 'The Lady' now that the Art Institute had decreed the portrait genuine. It's convenient that things turned out as they did so you and Anthony can save Hamilton Corporation and live happily ever after. By all means, take good care of your painting, but why should you care about me?"

A flicker of either coolly controlled fury or unbridled pain showed in the depths of his blue eyes as he pushed the carefully wrapped portrait into her hands. "This is neither the time nor the place to discuss it, Paige," he told her with ruthless severity. "I'm going now to get a cab, and if you and that portrait aren't here when I get back, I swear to God I'll call the police."

He turned away without another word and plunged from the sheltering archway into the downpour, unfurling his umbrella only as an afterthought. His shrill, ear-splitting whistle brought a taxi screeching to a halt at the foot of the steps, and she had no time to even consider escaping before Grant was coming back to collect her. His fingers were hard and uncompromising on her arm, and his face was set as he bundled first her and then the painting into the back seat of the cab. Once he had taken his place beside them, Grant gave the address.

"The Wickliffe Apartments on Lake Shore Drive," he said.

CHAPTER
Eleven

PAIGE TURNED HER face into the shower's spray as wisps of steam eddied around her. Grant had been right; the hot shower was dispelling the rain's chill, and she was feeling warmer. But for all the comfort she found in this watery haven, it could do nothing to assuage her terrible disappointment at the Art Institute's findings and her fear for the future.

When Richard Robusto had verified "The Lady of Dordrect" as Frans Hals's work, she had been too stunned to do more than stare stupidly, but now the enormity of that discovery washed over her with debilitating force. She had staked her hard-won reputation on the allegations that the portrait was a fake, but her claims had been refuted. How could she possibly have been so wrong? How could the results of Evan's procedures have been proved incorrect?

Feeling a noose of tears tighten around her throat, she stubbornly fought against them. She had been so sure about "The Lady," so confident of her claims, but today the tests had proved her wrong. She had used her well-honed skills to build a case against "The Lady of Dordrect," and she had been utterly mistaken. Though she couldn't grasp how she could have made such an error, her belief in herself as well as her credibility and reputation were gone. She had lost a job in the field she loved, without a hope of securing another, and she had been humiliated before her peers. What could the future possibly hold for her?

As she stood beneath the spray, Paige felt utterly desolate—without the work that was her life, without the man she'd come to love. Her mind closed in on blankness, and for a little while she was content to concentrate on nothing more than soaping her trailing hair and feeling the suds surge between her fingers, on sliding a slender bar of scented soap along her limbs and across her breasts and belly. She lost herself in those simple acts, listening to the crackle of the soapsuds in her ears and watching the shimmering bubbles trail along her body.

Grant's voice broke into her deliberately mundane thoughts. "You can't stay in there for the rest of your life, Paige," he warned her.

Through the frosted-glass door of the shower enclosure she could see his rippled silhouette. "Oh, can't I?" she asked almost plaintively.

"No, you can't. Come on, dry off. I've ordered us something to eat."

It was a full half hour later before she came to stand in the doorway of the living room, wrapped in one of the fluffy terry-cloth robes the apartment-hotel provided. She had paid little attention to the place when Grant had brought her in, hustling her through the main part of the apartment to the bedroom and bathroom beyond, but now her eyes swept appreciatively over the elegantly spare furnishings and the wall of windows, which on a clearer day would give a panoramic view of Lake Michigan.

So as not to detract from the scene beyond the windows, the furniture was simple: A gray modular couch was clustered in a semicircle in front of the fireplace at the south end of the room, where a fire burned brightly in the grate. At the other end stood a free-form plate-glass table and four sleek chairs. The table's wooden base was carved to follow the undulations in the wood's grain and burnished to a rich, tawny finish that gave it the texture of oozing caramel syrup. A few chrome-framed prints decorated the walls, but the view of Lake Michigan provided the focal point of the room.

When Paige came in, Grant glanced up from his copy of *The Chicago Tribune*. His shirt was open at the throat, and his cuffs were rolled back, emphasizing the contrast of his tanned forearms against the stark whiteness. His eyes followed her speculatively as she took a seat at the end of the curved couch opposite him and drew the terry-cloth robe more closely around her.

"Are you feeling better now?" he asked, watching her.

"Yes, I'm much warmer, thank you."

His lips thinned at her response; that wasn't what he wanted to know. He tried again. "You're sure you're all right?"

"Yes, I doubt very much if my soaking will give me a cold." She was being purposefully obtuse so she wouldn't have to discuss the forgery with him, and his exasperation was obvious.

She heard him draw a long breath and expel it in resignation. "I sent your clothes down to be dry-cleaned," he told her. "They should be back before too long."

She stirred slightly and pushed back a lock of still-damp hair. "I appreciate that," she mumbled.

"And I ordered us a special dinner, too. Since we're stranded here until tomorrow, I figured we should make the best of it."

"Did you order it to celebrate the Art Institute's findings?" she inquired caustically, then rose without waiting

Portrait of a Lady

for his answer and moved to the far end of the apartment.

The silence was brittle and sharp edged as she stood braced against the window, watching the quiver of lightning farther up the shore. Although her back was to Grant, she was very aware of his presence. The crinkle of the newspaper as he read seemed loud in the enveloping quiet, and she fought to keep from watching him in the glass's mirrorlike surface. Their mutual stubbornness held them immobile until there was a knock on the door and Grant went to answer it.

In the rain-spattered window's dark reflection Paige saw the waiter lay the table, taking candles, a bouquet of purple asters, and a wine bucket from his cart before he set out their plates, silverware, and wineglasses. The serving dishes came next—elegant, shiny domed platters, their polished covers clouded from the heat of the steaming food.

When the waiter was gone, Grant approached her. "Paige, please come and have something to eat."

Steeling herself to face him, she turned and took the place beside his. The cold, succulent shrimp in their tangy sauce might have been straw and the crisp, chilled wine water for all the pleasure she took in them. She ate with single-minded diligence, more for diversion than enjoyment.

When she had finished the shrimp cocktail, Grant raised the covers from the other dishes. "Chateaubriand? Broccoli in hollandaise? Duchess potatoes?" he tempted her, but Paige sat immobile, staring at her plate.

Then slow, searing tears began to seep from beneath her lowered lashes. She cried for some moments in silence, her icy demeanor denying Grant any right to comfort her.

"Oh, damn, I didn't mean to do this," she croaked miserably. "If you'll excuse me, Grant, I'm really not hungry."

She rose, intent on escaping to the bedroom, but he was swiftly beside her, catching both her arms.

"Oh, my poor darling," he soothed, drawing her close. "I know finding out 'The Lady of Dordrect' is a genuine

Hals has been a shock and disappointment, but it isn't the end of the world."

Angrily, with a single twist, she wrenched out of his arms. "Oh, isn't it, Grant?" she demanded, tears spilling down her face. "Do you have any idea how hard I worked for the position I have today and how much I love what I'm doing? Do you know how many dishes I washed in a grimy cafeteria, how many uninspired papers I typed, how many library books I shelved to get my education? Did you watch my mother scrimping to provide money for my schooling? Do you realize that all those years of struggle and effort were irrevocably destroyed today?"

He was stunned by her unleashed anger, shocked by her words of defeat. Was it possible the Art Institute's findings were as damning as she said? "I'm sorry about the bargain I made with Anthony," he apologized inadequately. "I was a fool to ever agree. I was sure the portrait was a forgery and convinced your job was secure. But even as things stand, can't you find a position in another museum?"

Paige shook her head passionately, her distress and agitation growing. "You don't know, Grant! You can't even begin to understand. No museum will hire me now!"

He tried to dismiss what she said as half-hysterical exaggeration, but no one was more realistic than Paige. "Damn it, Paige! No, I don't know. I don't understand. I haven't had much experience with the art world. Please, help me understand what's happened. If it concerns you, I want to know."

He curled one arm around her and drew her resisting body to the divan at the opposite end of the room. The firelight shown in the wetness on her cheeks and gilded her thick, clumped lashes. She had never seemed more vulnerable.

"Now, Paige, tell me. Please, tell me. I need so much to know."

His words touched her in a way she thought she'd steeled herself against, and she began to explain. It was difficult to make him see the differences between her world and his. He dealt in absolutes: in tests run, in formulas proved, in things that could be gauged and measured. That was why he had so docilely accepted the results of Evan's tests, why he had believed that the Art Institute's report would be redundant and useless. But she had known how imprecise and subjective the art world could be, how fragile and ephemeral her reputation was within it. In the next half hour she struggled to make him understand the shadowy sphere of conjecture and opinion, of brilliance and intuition, she lived in every day. And when she was quiet at last, they huddled together before the fire: Paige spent and limp, grateful for the bulwark of his shoulder to lean on, Grant enlightened and troubled.

As she spoke, the choices he had to weigh became abundantly clear to him. He could acknowledge "The Lady of Dordrect" as a genuine Hals and keep Hamilton Corporation from ruin, or he could save the reputation of the woman he loved. If he had only himself to consider, the answer would be easy, but there was so much more to it. He had employees, the stockholders, the board of directors, and Anthony to answer to, and they all lobbied noisily in his head. He had to consider the economic welfare of the state and the new European contacts. How could he turn his back on those responsibilities in favor of one, lone woman, no matter how much he loved her? He could lose his company, his fortune, and all he had worked to attain, or he could sacrifice Paige Fenton. It was a decision Grant didn't know how to make.

Unaware of his struggle, Paige nestled closer. He felt the brush of her cinnamon hair against his cheek, felt the press of her unbound breasts against him, and he was lost. As irrational as he knew it was to try to suppress the Art Institute's report, he would not see Paige destroyed because of it, could not stand idly by and let her lose everything.

Pulling free of her clinging arms, he surged to his feet and bolted toward the coat rack in the hall. He brushed past the portrait without a second glance and rummaged through the pockets of his blazer. The report was in the second one, and he returned to the main room in triumph. He didn't give a damn about the consquences. He only knew he must destroy the Art Institute's report and keep the secret of their findings forever.

Paige rose as he recrossed the room. "What is it, Grant? What's the matter?"

Without a word of explanation he stared at the flickering fire. Then, as she saw the papers in his hand, she realized what he meant to do. Reacting without thinking, she whirled to place her body between the report and the flames. They struggled for a moment in silence, his hands hard and rough in his determination to complete what he had begun. Seeing at once that her strength was no match for his, Paige used the only tactic that could deter him.

Murmuring his name, she slipped her arms around his neck and brought her scantily clad body full against him. The lushness of her femininity flowed along the length of his rigid form, and, as always, the contact was charged with excitement, provocation, and something more. Caught between his own intentions and Paige's insidious blockade, Grant shuddered to a halt, his determination dissipated, nullified by the force of his conflicting emotions.

Paige continued to assault his senses, tracing slowly expanding patterns across his broad back as she pressed kisses along his throat. She felt the tremor of his pulse beneath her lips as his arms came almost grudgingly around her. His will to fight slowly ebbed away, and he turned his face into her fragrant hair as his ragged breathing slowed. They stood locked together for a long time like two sides of an arch, each holding the other erect. Finally Grant raised his head.

"Why didn't you let me do it?" he asked. "Why wouldn't you let me destroy the Art Institute's report? You wouldn't be in this position except for me."

One of her hands stroked the soft, sun-streaked hair that grew long on his collar while the other plucked the papers from his lax fingers and tucked them safely into the pocket of her robe. "As much as I'm touched by what you tried to do," she answered, "I couldn't live the rest of my life based on a lie. I was wrong about 'The Lady'; somehow I was mistaken about her being a forgery. As hard as that is to accept, it's something I must do. We all have to live with the consequences of our mistakes, and if I never work as a conservator again, I'll survive somehow. This isn't your fault, Grant. You mustn't blame yourself."

An unspeakable weariness melted Grant's bones, and he slumped heavily against her. He hadn't stopped to consider what she would want or how she would feel if he destroyed the report. Paige was a woman of impeccable integrity and unquenchable pride. How could he expect her to live with his lie?

Surely, when he took the time to think about it, there were other copies of the Art Institute's findings, other people who would expose his deception to the world. He'd made a grandiose gesture: all show and no substance. His head sank to her shoulder, and he accepted from her the comfort he had expected to give.

"I'm sorry," he whispered against her ear, defeated, exhausted, spent.

He felt her cheek move against him as her lips grazed his brow. "Grant?" she asked after a moment. "Grant?" He raised his head. "Why did you do it? Why did you try to burn the report?"

"I did it because I love you, Paige," he said simply. "Because I love you."

He saw the sheen of fresh tears on her lashes as she raised her mouth to his. "Grant," she murmured. "Grant." She kissed him again. "Oh, Grant, I love you, too." The third kiss was equally tender, but deeper, more committed, filled with longing. It swelled with growing emotion as her hands came up to bracket his face, her thumbs tracing the line of his cheekbones. With leisurely thoroughness she explored the wide, generous shape of his lips and the warm, welcoming depths of his mouth. Her fingers tangled in his tousled hair and stroked down across his neck and shoulders, soothing him, easing him, releasing in him the last coils of residual opposition.

Grant stood entranced and immobile, trusting and pliant, secure enough within himself and in his love for Paige to relinquish the role he had been taught a man should play. He succumbed willingly to the sweet sorcery in her touch, the sensuous delight of her teasing tongue curling and flicking against his. Her soft breath mingled with his own as their kisses deepened with careless abandon. The wondrous enchantment grew within him as his thoughts blurred to nothingness and his awareness of his surroundings slipped away.

Paige continued to weave her relentless spell of devastating physical sensation until his only reality was his delight in her nearness. Still kissing him, she unfastened his shirt buttons and gently moved her splayed fingers over his heated flesh, outlining the rugged musculature that was clearly defined by the fire's amber glow. By minute degrees her lips moved across his cheek to his ear, where she nibbled provoatively at the lobe before exploring the concave inner turnings with her tongue.

A ragged moan of desire rose in his throat as ripples of escalating need shuddered through him. Paige smiled to herself as she pressed an unbroken chain of open-mouthed kisses along the column of his throat and across one shoulder, pausing at last to swirl concentric circles over his breast bone. Beneath her lips his heart beat rapidly.

"Oh, Paige, my love, my darling," he murmured dazedly, raising her chin with one trembling hand to afford him access to her mouth. The kiss he pressed upon her was hot and erotic, tense with the pain of frustrated longing. It went on and on, gentle yet determined, harsh and tender, drawing them both into the vortex of budding desire. When he raised his head at last to stare into her eyes, she was clearly as bewitched as he. She took his hand and led him toward the bedroom.

At that moment Grant could not have resisted her touch if she were a siren leading him to his doom instead of a lover inviting him to the esctasy of exquisite passion. He was totally committed to this woman in all her forms: conscientious professional, sharp-tongued nemesis, understanding confidant, uninhibited bedmate. He loved Paige with a depth and constancy he had never before experienced.

Once in the dimly lit bedroom, she undressed him, sliding the oxford-cloth shirt down his arms, skimming the gray flannel trousers and underwear along his legs. He sank to the edge of the bed and drew Paige to stand between his thighs. Her robe had fallen open, and he slid his hands around her waist beneath the gaping fabric, intensely aware of its rough texture in contrast to her silken skin. Like a supplicant worshiping her sleek body, he pressed reverent kisses in the warm, mysterious valley between her breasts. Nuzzling the cloth aside, he bared one nipple and took the rosy tip between his lips. He heard her swift indrawn breath of anticipation and sensed the shudder of response that moved along her spine as her flesh grew slick and taut against his tongue. Holding her close, he felt more ripples spread along her limbs, their intensity fueling the growing need that spiraled through him.

Looking down at the dark head pressed against her bosom, Paige gave in to her own desire. With no wish to resist him, she let the terry-cloth robe crumple to the floor and threaded her fingers through his hair. In the dimness she saw the rugged muscles beneath his tawny skin strain and shift as he pulled her down beside him on the bed. His big body curved protectively and possessively to enfold her.

She lay passive for a moment, staring up into his shining eyes, entranced, enraptured, lost in the depth and wonder of his love. His kisses moved over her with the gentle insistence of a spring rain, like an astringent on the sensitive skin of her face and throat, pooling in the hollows of her wrists and elbows. He courted her with kisses, lavishing on her his most tender caresses, proving over and over his delight, his desire, and his love for her.

His hand trailed down across her belly to the mound of soft red hair between her thighs and lay there for a moment as her heat rose up against his palm. Then he probed deep into the moist, willing recess of her femininity. Paige twisted in a turmoil of response, but Grant gentled her with his mouth and touch until she lay mesmerized by the sweetness of the mounting sensation. Her lips moved against his throat as he stroked deeper and deeper, until her need to touch and hold him grew beyond all bounds.

Her trembling fingers found what she was seeking, and she matched his movements stroke for stroke. When the delight grew too much to bear, Grant's body molded to the shape of hers, conforming to every curve, and with a thrill of remembered rapture he found a haven deep inside. The exquisite sensations of that eager joining took their breath as they lay still, staring into each other's eyes, joyous and united.

"I love you, Paige. I love you," Grant whispered as he began to move within her, circling and then pressing deep, a slave to his suddenly raging desire. Paige answered his need with a hunger of her own, arching against him, sundering his control.

The world seemed to glow with the reflected intensity of their perfect passion, as if warmed and renewed by the power of their love. They were swelling and bursting with the sweet energy inside them, a unifying fire that could not be contained. It flared up within them, and they clung together for those exquisite moments, bathed in an aura of intimacy more overpowering and profound than anything they'd ever known. They were bound together irrevocably by the fervor of their emotions, their hearts, minds, and bodies mystically melded into one. And even as the surge of ravishing sensation died away, they were left complete

Portrait of a Lady

and whole, forged eternally together.

A long time later they were roused by the rumble of thunder across Chicago and by the shimmy of lightning outside their windows. Grant stirred sluggishly to pull up the rumpled covers, tucking them solicitously around Paige before snuggling down beside her. With his head pillowed against her shoulder and her arm draped comfortably around him, he nuzzled her neck.

"I love you, Paige," he murmured, his voice throaty, soft, and low.

"And I love you, Grant. I love you very much."

He was very nearly purring with contentment as she drew lazy circles on his back with one finger.

"Grant?" she whispered. "Grant?"

"Mmm."

"Would you still love me if 'The Lady of Dordrect' was a fake?" she asked, her mind still busy with the puzzle she couldn't solve.

She sensed his smile in the darkness. "Of course I'd still love you. It would just be a lot harder to prove it to you." He sounded smug, self-assured, and drowsy, and by the time she had framed a suitably witty reply, he had fallen asleep.

Paige lay awake beside him, turning the question of the Hals portrait over and over in her mind. How could she have so misjudged the painting, been so utterly wrong about its origins? What flaw in Evan's testing had the Art Institute's experts found that even she had not discovered?

Knowing she couldn't rest until she understood their findings, she slipped her arm from around Grant and squirmed toward the edge of the bed. He stirred and mumbled something in his sleep, but by the time she had located her robe and slipped it on, his breathing was deep and regular once more.

She cast a final glance at his sleeping form and smiled to herself before stepping into the living room. Finding her way by the gutting candles on the table and the barely glowing embers of the fire, she crossed the dim apartment to stand beside the windows, her thoughts low-keyed and cool.

Whatever she had thought today would bring, her imaginings were far different from the reality. She had never expected Grant to declare his love for her, never suspected that her career would be destroyed. She turned her mind readily to the first thought, the far happier one to contemplate, and remembered Grant's words of love, the perfection of their passion.

"I love you, Paige. I love you," he had whispered almost hypnotically. Paige was touched and warmed by the memory. She wouldn't mind hearing those words at least a dozen times every day for the rest of her life. But then, Grant had only spoken of his feelings for her this evening, and perhaps it wasn't wise to think beyond the moments they'd just shared.

But why? Was she refusing to consider a commitment to Grant because she feared what would happen tomorrow? Something stubborn and indomitable deep inside her rose up to shout the denial. No, she wasn't afraid of the future, and she would make her own way in the world, with or without Grant. She loved him, and she would gladly spend the rest of her life with him, if he asked her. But she would accept him on her own terms, not because she was a poor, disenfranchised waif without a job, without prospects, taken in out of pity. She was her own woman and always would be, taking responsibility for herself, her career, and her mistakes.

Then a totally stunning thought streaked across her consciousness, nearly overwhelming her new-found confidence. Tonight she and Grant had shared an intimacy and intensity of emotion beyond anything she'd ever known. They'd made exquisite and impassioned love without considering anything but those wild, sweet moments of delight. Lost in that all-encompassing bliss, they had not taken even the most basic precautions. Grant had left his seed inside her, and if fate willed it, she would bear his child.

Even through her doubts and uncertainties, that possibility lit a warm, insistent glow inside her. She loved Grant wholeheartedly and unselfishly. She loved him and wanted his child, now or sometime in the future.

Running a hand through her tumbled hair, she stared out at the huge black lake. The beacon far out in the harbor was making its unending circuit, flashing its warning across the storm-tossed water. She drew a long breath and let it out slowly. She hadn't left the comfort of the bed or the warmth of Grant to contemplate the uncertain future, but to discover her past mistakes.

Drawing the Art Institute's report from the pocket of her robe, she turned from the windows, switched on a light, and curled up on the couch to study its contents. She had read and reread Evan's report so many times that she knew his graceful phrases by heart: "The crevicelike craquelure," "the paint's impossibly vibrant hures," "the work of a skilled but mundane artisan."

The Art Institute's report was drier but more to the point, their tests minutely documented. As she read over the typed pages, her carefully trained mind began to pick out strange discrepancies between the two groups of findings. The lead content in the white paint was far higher in the Art Institute's tests, the descriptions of the brush strokes varied sharply, and the analysis of the dust accumulation in the cracks of the paint were totally at odds. It was almost as if the two museums had analyzed completely different portraits.

Tossing the papers aside, Paige went to where the painting stood against the wall in the foyer. She wouldn't be satisfied until she'd examined "The Lady of Dordrect" again herself. Moving it with utmost care, she carried it into the living room, then switched on all the lights.

Gingerly, she broke the seal on the outer wrappings and peeled away the alternating layers of packing and protective cardboard until "The Lady of Dordrect" lay on the onyx-topped table before her. The Lady's cool gray eyes smiled up at her, twinkling with an inner light; the perfectly bowed mouth seemed ready to whisper a secret; the jade green ring was brilliant on her slender hand; and the Brussels lace cap looked fragile and incredibly intricate.

Never in her lab had the Hals prortrait looked so lovely and elegant, so fresh and vital, so golden and serene. Not once in all the times she'd looked at it had she felt this strange catch in her chest or felt the small hairs stir along her arms. It was a portrait of exquisite warmth and beauty, and Paige knew without examining it further that she'd been wrong. This painting was unquestionably a Frans Hals masterpiece.

Still, a pragmatic part of her demanded further examination. Taking a small magnifying glass from her purse, Paige carefully perused the surface. It was flawless, with the warm, rich glow that so typified Dutch and Flemish work. From what she could tell, even the dust collected in the minute cracks was everything it should be. Lifting the portrait almost reverently, she turned it to the light, squinting past the sheen of varnish to study the portrait's surface.

Suddenly her heart lurched to a stop, then resumed beating double time. Paige herself had removed every speck of the old varnish from "The Lady of Dordrect," and with Evan away, no one could have replaced it. Yet this painting had its protective layer of varnish intact!

With exaggerated care she returned the painting to the table and sat huddled on the couch, clenching her trembling hands together.

This painting wasn't the "The Lady of Dordrect" she had packed at the Tri-City Museum just that morning. That painting was a fake; this one was genuine. Still, her mind rejected the conclusion as assiduously as it had rejected the discovery she had made a week before. In spite of what she knew with every fiber of her being, she needed more proof.

Slowly she turned the portrait over, searching for the accession number on the back. At the time of purchase or bequest, each piece of art acquired by a museum was marked by a number to catalog it and help keep track of it within the museum. "The Lady of Dordrect" had been assigned number 132:1984—the one hundred and thirty-second object to have been acquired by the Tri-City Art Museum that year. The number had been placed on the lower-left corner of the portrait, on the back of the stretcher; she had noticed it repeatedly as she'd worked. But now, though she searched every inch of the wood, she couldn't find the accession number. Two identical pictures, one genuine and one fake, had obviously been switched!

The *why* was easy to explain; someone was trying to defraud the museum. The more pressing question was: *when* and *by whom* had the exchange been accomplished? Grant, the thought intruded, but Paige quickly forced it away, dishonored by her suspicion. Grant had proved himself honest and trustworthy. He loved her and would never do anything to harm her.

Who else could possibly have had a chance to exchange the fake for the genuine? Before her suspicion could blossom into full-blown doubt, Paige headed for the bedroom.

"Grant! Grant! You must wake up!" she implored him, switching on the bedside lamp.

He came awake with a start, immediately alert. "What is it, Paige? What's the matter?" He reached across to catch her hand, the touch reassuring them both.

"The painting in the living room," she poured out. "'The Lady of Dordrect' is really a Frans Hals."

His eyes were filled with confusion as he took in her adamant expression. "Yes, Paige, I know," he assured her. "The Art Institute confirmed that 'The Lady' is genuinely Frans Hals's work. Why are you waking me up in the middle of the night to tell me something that's already been proven?"

She shook her head in agitation. "No, no. Grant, you don't understand. There are two paintings of 'The Lady of Dordrect,' one real and one fake, and somehow they've been switched!" Swiftly and concisely she explained what she'd found. "As impossible as it seems, that's what must have happened. But when were the paintings exchanged, and who could be behind this deception?"

Grant had been growing steadily paler as she revealed more and more of her discovery. In answer to her question he breathed a single name: "Anthony!"

CHAPTER
Twelve

PAIGE AWOKE BY slow degrees, becoming gradually aware of the *whoosh* of tires on the rain-slicked pavement, of the late-night disk jockey's purring voice on the radio, of the continuous grumble of distant thunder. A current of cold air licked across her bared throat, chilling her and she felt stiff and uncomfortable from having fallen asleep sitting up.

"Where are we?" she asked as she stirred against the seat cushions and stretched.

"About an hour from Riverview," Grant informed her, piloting the rental car skillfully around a sharply banked curve. Paige glanced across at him with a swell of concern; she'd slept much longer than she'd intended.

"Why don't you let me drive for a while, Grant? You must be getting tired." In the reflected light from the dashboard his face did seem pale and drawn.

His attention never left the road, his eyes locked on the slick surface. "No, I'm fine."

His reply was almost brusque, and Paige realized he'd said scarcely a dozen words since they'd left Chicago just after two A.M. Once Grant had fully understood the scope of her discovery concerning "The Lady of Dordrect," his decision to leave the city had been implacable. They would hire a rental car and drive the several hundred miles to confront Anthony at Riverview rather than wait for the weather to clear so they could fly.

While Paige had dressed in her freshly laundered clothes, Grant had arranged for a car to be gassed up and waiting for them when they emerged from the apartment building. As the suburbs had fallen behind them, the silence in the car and the late hour had taken their toll, and Paige had fallen asleep.

Now, as they sped through the flat midwestern landscape, Paige watched Grant carefully, trying to discern his thoughts. His chiseled profile was dark against the gradually lightening sky, and in the rigid set of his beard-stubbled jaw and his narrowly compressed lips she sensed the grim misery bottled up inside him. His hands were clamped around the steering wheel in a deliberate grip that communicated tension through his entire body.

Clearly Anthony's cunning deception concerning "The Lady of Dordrect" had wounded Grant deeply, but beyond the pain of his brother's betrayal was a dangerous, slow-burning anger that Paige had never before seen in Grant. During their brief but intimate relationship his bouts of temper had been as fierce and fleeting as summer storms, but this brooding indignation was far different from those noisy outbursts. It was like water rushing through a narrow river channel, all the more turbulent and treacherous for being confined. Instinctively, Paige understood that she must find a way to divert his focus and diffuse his hostility before they reached the estate at Riverview, or face the inevitable consequences of Grant's unleashed wrath.

Portrait of a Lady

He was holding her at arm's length with his bitterness and reticence, his anger and confusion. Yet the cool, impersonal distance he had put between them was an obstacle she would not allow. Last night in Chicago he had demanded that she open herself to him and share her fears and problems. Now she was unwilling to accept anything less from him.

"Grant," she began as she switched off the radio, determined to have his full attention, "even since we left Chicago, I've been wondering about something."

Before answering, he pulled into the left lane to pass a slower car. "What?"

"I've been trying to figure out just how Anthony managed to switch the two portraits without drawing attention to his actions. Do you know how he did it?" The question wasn't as much to the point as Paige would have liked, but it opened a discussion between them.

Grant reacted as if she had stormed the last bastion of his privacy. He glanced away from the road for a long moment, a forbidding frown between his brows. "I really don't want to discuss it, Paige," he growled.

She registered his obvious disapproval, but tried again. "Don't you suppose Anthony must have had an accomplice to make his plan work, someone who could actually exchange the portraits without arousing undue suspicion?" She paused, trying to gauge his expression, then continued as if she were only thinking aloud. "It seems safe to assume that no one at the Art Institute is involved in the deception. But if that's so, the only other people who had access to the paintings, besides the two of us, were the chauffeur who drove us to the airport and the pilot of the corporate jet who helped me secure the painting for our flight to Chicago."

Grant stirred uncomfortably. "I told you I'm not interested in this kind of idle speculation," he warned her.

"But, Grant, aren't you the least bit curious to know how the switch was done?" Her persistence was paying off; she could sense his mounting irritation. "Which one of those two men actually completed the transaction? And do you think whoever did it planned to exchange the portraits a second time so I would return to the Tri-City Museum with the fake instead of with the genuine Hals?"

Grant considered her question in silence, trying to resist the urge to indulge in his own speculation. He didn't want to know too much about the exchange of the two portraits; he didn't want to understand the means of Anthony's betrayal. Still, against his will, his mind sought out the answers. "It must have been Briggs, the chauffeur, who switched the portraits," he admitted at last. "He's been with the family for years and years, and is totally loyal to Anthony." He spoke with a tone of ruthless finality, obviously hoping Paige would end her unwelcome probing. She did not.

"But how could Anthony be sure you were going to take the limo to the airfield?" she persisted. "That isn't the normal way you would have come to get me, is it?"

Paige was acutely aware that Grant's suppressed anger was seeping toward the surface. The muscles in his arms were flexed and tight beneath the thin fabric of his shirt, and she felt the car accelerate as he pressed still harder on the gas pedal.

"No, of course that's not the way I would normally have come to get you," he snapped. "Any other time I'd have taken the roadster, or, considering that we had to transport the painting, I'd have come in the company's Wagoneer."

"Then why did you pick me up in the limousine instead?"

His mouth quirked down in one corner, but he didn't look at her. "I took the limo because I was in no condition to drive. Or didn't you notice?"

Paige turned to watch him closely, wondering what he meant. His actions the previous morning had been out of the ordinary, but she had ascribed his behavior to the animosity between them rather than to any external cause. "I admit you were hardly yourself, Grant. But why weren't you able to drive to the museum to get me?"

"I really doubt this has any bearing on what we've been discussing," he muttered, still trying to deter her. "I think you're wrong in trying to make this situation more complex than it is."

Paige continued watching him, aware of his evasions. Just what was he so determined to hide? "Why don't you simply explain your decision to take the limo and let me be the judge of its importance?"

His already formidable frown deepened with derision and self-disgust. "I took the limo for the same reason I failed to call you Wednesday night—because I was totally, inexcusably drunk!"

Paige could hardly give credence to his words. "Drunk!" she gasped. "Grant! I've never known anyone to be as careful about alcohol as you!"

"Getting drunk isn't a pastime I usually enjoy," he admitted, "and I'm not very proud of my behavior. I'm not even sure how it happened. Anthony had only just poured our second Scotch when the drinks began to hit me."

Paige was puzzled, too. The two times she'd seen Grant drink he had consumed far more liquor than that without any hint of intoxication. Then, at his innocent observation, a terrible suspicion began to grow inside her. She was almost afraid to tell Grant what she was thinking. Could Anthony have put a drug in that first glass of Scotch to ensure Grant would be incapable of driving the next morning?

With a chill of intuition, she was sure he had. But she was justly apprehensive about voicing her conviction, knowing full well that the charge could hurt their burgeoning love. "Is it possible," she finally asked in a very low tone, "that Anthony put something in that first glass besides whiskey?"

Grant's head snapped around as if she'd shouted the accusation, disbelief and acknowledgment evident in his widening eyes. Before he gave an answer, he pulled the car onto the shoulder of the road and stopped it, then sat staring straight ahead, stunned and devastated.

Paige let him sit in silence for as long as she could bear it, then reached across to touch his rigid arm. "Grant?" she whispered. "Grant?"

"So you think my own brother drugged me to promote his sinister plans? Well, Anthony wouldn't. Anthony couldn't do anything to hurt me. He couldn't be that . . . that devious and calculating!" His tortured voice filled the car, ricocheting off the glass as he roared the denial. Then he slumped over the steering wheel, his head against his tightly clenched fists. He was breathing as if he'd run a hundred miles, his chest expanding and contracting sharply as he fought the overwhelming truth.

Without hesitation Paige reached out to comfort him, sliding across the wide seat to take him in her arms. She needed to do something to assuage his pain, to lessen the anguish of his disillusionment. Offering all the compassion within her, she pulled him close and saw, as he turned to accept her consolation, that his eyes were wet with tears.

"Oh, Paige. I tried so hard to win Anthony's approval," he rasped against her shoulder, putting his feelings for his brother into words at last. "I wanted so much for us to be able to work together. I hoped that eventually a partnership would evolve. There was room in the company for both of us. I thought that in time he'd stop seeing me as a threat and realize that by jointly controling Hamilton Corporation, we could make it stronger and more productive."

The confession seemed to erupt from deep inside Grant, from painful old wounds and festering uncertainties that had never had a chance to heal. Concern for the man she loved swept through Paige as he spoke, and she wept for his grief as if it were her own.

"I . . . I love Anthony," Grant conceded. "I love him, and all I ever really wanted was his acceptance and a chance to take my rightful place in the family and in the company."

Paige's tears fell freely, dripping into his hair as she hugged him close. She felt the wetness of his own tears hot and soft against her throat. They clung together tightly, Paige offering Grant hope in the midst of disillusionment and calm in the depth of confusion. In that long and quiet moment she cared for Grant with a fierce, protective passion as primitive and basic as love itself.

She held him for what seemed like an eternity in the hazy dawn, crooning to him softly, trying to ease his pain. What she said to him she hardly knew herself: words of sympathy and compassion, of love and reassurance. They came from some unexpected wellspring of tenderness deep within her heart that, until she knew and loved Grant, she had never tapped.

The rain had stopped, and a sliver of orange sun was peeping over the eastern horizon when Grant finally raised his head. She could see he was exhausted, but the terrible tension and intensity that had filled him had somehow ebbed away.

Paige smiled up into his eyes, searching for and finding the strength and resilience that had always been part of him. "What are we going to do now?" she asked.

He took a long breath and expelled it slowly. "I don't know," he admitted, shaking his head. "Before I face Anthony, I feel I must find proof of our suspicions, and the only way to get that is to continue on to Riverview. Does that make sense to you?"

"Confronting Anthony makes the only sense," Paige agreed quietly.

With the hint of a smile Grant bent his head to kiss her, tasting deeply of her sweetness before breaking off the embrace.

"I love you, Paige, with all my heart," he whispered gently, then determinedly turned away to start the car again.

By the time they reached Riverview, it was full daylight. Across the glistening, rain-soaked lawns the main house glowed in the warm amber sunlight. Grant drove past the impressive eastern facade to the hollow beyond the gardens where the stone garages stood. As they moved stealthily through one of the dim structures, Paige was aware of the panoply of vehicles housed there: a forest-green Jaguar sedan, a 1948 Rolls-Royce, a sporty red Maserati. At the end of the line crouched the sleek black limousine, its body and chrome polished to a dazzling sheen. With the keys Grant found dangling in the ignition he quietly unlocked the trunk. Beneath the crimson folds of a woolly Harvard blanket, a carefully wrapped parcel lay concealed.

"Do you think that's it?" Paige ventured in a whisper.

"Unless I miss my guess," he whispered back. "It's the right size, isn't it?"

As Grant bent to lift the forgery from its hiding place, a stern, masculine voice sounded close behind them. "Just what do you think you're doing poking around in here?"

Paige whirled to face the speaker and found herself staring down the barrel of a snub-nosed pistol. Her exclamation of alarm brought Grant erect beside her, and when the slight, elderly man recognized him, he let the muzzle of the gun sag toward the floor.

"You're pretty heavily armed for a trip to the garages, aren't you, Briggs?" Grant inquired dryly. For the first time Paige noticed the trim, dark uniform the man wore.

"I'm terribly sorry, Mister Grant," the chauffeur apologized. "I saw a strange car drive in and was afraid you were intruders. Mister Anthony told me he didn't expect you back until late this afternoon."

"Yes, I imagine Anthony will be surprised to see us," Grant agreed. "Do you know anything about this package in the trunk?"

The older man's face went brilliant red. "Package?" he mumbled with a nervous shudder, refusing to meet Grant's eyes.

"Yes, Briggs," Grant continued. "A parcel just about the size and shape of 'The Lady of Dordrect.'"

Briggs squirmed as Grant reached inside the trunk to get the portrait. "I'd say this looks a great deal like the package we took with us to Chicago, wouldn't you, Paige? The one that contains the genuine painting of 'The Lady of Dordrect'?"

The chauffeur's flushed face had gone ashen, and he fumbled for an explanation. "I...I didn't want...Mister Anthony said..."

"Save your excuses, Briggs," Grant snapped, his finely molded face like polished granite. "We're aware of what's been done. Lock that pistol in the office; you're coming to the house with us."

A few minutes later Grant left Paige, Briggs, and the two wrapped paintings in the foyer of the main house and disappeared into a room at the end of the hall. While they waited for him to return, Paige studied the terrified chauffeur, wondering how this unassuming little man had gotten swept up in Anthony's plotting. His guilt in switching the portraits was patently obvious in the compulsive way he rubbed his palms together and the sheen of sweat that glazed his upper lip. What kind of a bribe had Anthony offered him? What kind of lies had Anthony told him to gain his complicity in the affair?

Grant's reappearance put an end to Paige's musings as he showed her the prescription bottle he had found. "What is it?" she inquired so that only he could hear.

"They're sleeping pills," he muttered grimly. "Probably dangerous as hell when mixed with alcohol, too. The bottle was right there on the bar."

"Oh, Grant! I'm so sorry..." she began, but he waved her to silence.

"Now that I've got the proof I need, I think it's time to confront my brother." He stole a quick look at his watch. "He's probably still at breakfast in the dining room. Leave those things here and come along. I imagine he'll need to hear from all of us before he'll admit what he's done."

Paige followed close behind him, watching Grant with narrowed eyes. Since they had arrived at Riverview, he had been calm and coolly deliberate in his actions, but she wondered about his state of mind. What was he thinking and feeling now that the confrontation with Anthony was at hand? Knowing she could be no more than a witness to the forthcoming conflict filled her with incoherent dread. Would Grant be able to confront his brother and remain unscathed, or would she see the man she loved destroyed?

Grant burst into the large, elegantly furnished dining room, his entourage at his heels, and stopped to stand at the near end of the long mahogany table. His brother sat at the opposite end, poking idly into an egg cup as he read the morning paper.

"Good morning, Anthony," Grant greeted him. "I'm sorry to break in on your breakfast like this, but there's a matter of some importance we need to discuss. By the way, this is Miss Paige Fenton from the Tri-City Museum, and of course you already know our driver, Mr. Briggs."

Darker than Grant in both color and intent, Anthony looked up at the unexpected interruption of his morning meal and lifted one imperious eyebrow. His gaze flicked over them with marked contempt, taking in the minutest details.

Paige stared back just as intently. She remembered seeing him at art museum functions, but he had always been too busy with the power brokers and trustees of the institution to notice anyone as lowly as she. Her inventory of him was careful and complete; she took in the crisp waves of his dark hair, the obsidian eyes, the deepening lines of displeasure around his mouth, and the broad chest and shoulders visible where the expensive silk dressing gown gaped open. In some ways he was so like Grant, with the same compelling features. Yet there was a subtle weakness to his chin, a hint of pettiness in the shape of his lips, a frightening ruthlessness in his glare that negated all the similarities.

Paige knew she should hate Anthony for what he'd done to Grant, for defrauding the museum, for trying to destroy her career. But, oddly, all she felt was pity. In the instant when she recognized her feelings, her fear and anger dropped away, and she knew that, whatever happened in the next few minutes, Anthony had lost the power to hurt them.

"Well, Grant," Anthony said at last, laying aside his heavy linen napkin, "did the weather in Chicago clear more quickly than you expected? I didn't think you'd be back until this afternoon."

"No, Anthony, we drove in this morning. There were some discrepancies in the two museums' findings that I was very anxious to discuss with you."

"Discrepancies? Really?" he asked, seeming unconcerned. "What did the Art Institute discover?"

"They found that 'The Lady of Dordrect' we took to Chicago was a genuine Hals, just as you suspected." Grant paused, waiting for his brother's response. When Anthony only nodded, he continued. "But then, that's hardly surprising when you made certain the portrait they examined was indeed Hals's work."

"Well, of course it was, Grant. What else could it be?" he inquired, allowing himself a feral smile.

"It could have been a forgery," Grant suggested. "like the one you tried to pawn off on the Tri-City Museum."

"I haven't the slightest idea what you're talking about," Anthony answered. It was a barefaced lie, and Paige couldn't help but admire his cool delivery.

"I think you're quite aware of the existence of another copy of 'The Lady,' especially since we found her hidden in the trunk of the limo. It was there so that the portraits could be exchanged one last time when Briggs picked us up at the airfield."

"My God, Grant, you dare accuse your own brother of double-dealing?" Anthony fumed.

"Do you need to see proof of the charges?" Grant countered. "Very well, Anthony, Paige, Briggs, go get the portraits."

The two scrambled to comply with Grant's order, bringing in the two identical parcels, then stripping away the protective layers of paper and cardboard until the pair of portraits stood side by side braced against the dining room wall. As alike as they were, the differences between them were clear, like comparing gold to common stone. On the right, the Hals glowed with vigor and life, while the copy on the left remained nothing more than a clever imitation.

"So you see, Anthony, there are two," Grant pointed out. "Two paintings of the same woman, very much alike but worlds and centuries apart. Argenta examined the real one here before it was switched for the fake. When Paige discovered the forgery you sold to the museum, you made arrangements to have the paintings switched again before the Art Institute could verify her findings. And if I have the scenario correct, Briggs here was to exchange them one last time so the Tri-City Museum would end up with this worthless trash!"

Grant spun around as he spoke and put his foot through the counterfeit Hals. The crackle of shattering paint and the sound of rending canvas brought Anthony to his feet.

"This is preposterous!" he shouted. "Good God, just look what you've done. And every word you've said, Grant, every word is a lie!"

Grant turned to the elderly chauffeur. "What about it, Briggs?" he asked softly. "Are they lies, or does what I've said have a certain ring of truth?"

"Briggs!" Anthony's voice echoed in the paneled room and set the crystal chandelier tinkling.

The gray-haired man bobbed his head in affirmation. "That's pretty much the way of it, Mister Grant," he acknowledged. "But I only did it to help our Mister Anthony. I've been with your family for almost forty years, in one job or another, and the Hamiltons have always been good to me."

"That's enough, Briggs!" Anthony interjected, but the little chauffeur had a great deal more to say.

"When your brother came and told me that 'The Lady' was going to be donated to the museum and asked for my help in exchanging the two paintings, I said I'd do it. He said he loved that portrait as much as your mother had and that he was desperate to keep it in the family, but you were insisting on giving it to the museum. It's no secret to anyone who worked for the Hamiltons the store your mother set by that picture. I remember seeing her sit by the hour just watching the woman in the painting, as if they shared some special secret. She was a good, kind woman, your mother, though she favored one son too much. Anyway, I switched the paintings because of her and to keep 'The Lady' from being given away."

There was a long, solemn silence before Grant spoke, compelled to tell the chauffeur the truth. "'The Lady of Dordrect' wasn't donated, Briggs," he said softly. "It was sold to the Tri-City Museum for well over two million dollars." Taking a deep breath, Grant turned back to his brother, his face grave. "Well, Anthony," he said, "have you anything more to say before we go to the museum?"

Anthony's face was contorted with rage. "Yes, dammit, I have a great deal more to say. I really did want to keep 'The Lady' in the family. She's been in Hamilton hands for four generations, and I couldn't bear to see her fawned over by a bunch of common louts who could never appreciate her beauty. It's still not too late to continue with the plans I made. We can take the forgery to the museum and say she was damaged in transit. If she can't be restored by the conservation techniques they have today, there's always the insurance. We could collect a cool two million and still have the genuine Hals. Surely your little sweetheart can be bought off, and Briggs..."

Grant took the prescription bottle from his pocket and looked down at it before tossing it toward his brother. The vial skittered and rolled crazily along the length of the satiny mahogany table before it bounced off the edge and dropped to the floor.

"Why did you really do it?" Grant demanded.

Anthony's swarthy face went chalky as he stood facing his accuser, and when he spoke at last, his voice had lost its crispness. "I did it for a dozen reasons," he admitted. "I really did want to keep the painting in the family; it's where it belongs. But the way I arranged things before I left for Europe, if the forgery was discovered, the blame would fall on you. My plan couldn't fail: Either way I kept the genuine Hals. Then, too, there was the added incentive that you might be discredited and forced to resign from Hamilton Corporation. It was a well-laid plan, with alternatives and contingencies, a perfect set-up that would have succeeded brilliantly if it hadn't been for her!"

The hostility in the glare he fixed on Paige sent shivers down her spine, and she was glad when Grant stepped protectively closer.

"I think it's best if we all go to the Tri-City Museum together and tell Arthur Franklin what's happened. Briggs, go get the car," Grant ordered. "Anthony, you have twenty minutes to get dressed and ready." He paused to watch his brother before he continued. "And, Anthony, while I don't give a damn what Franklin does to you, let's hope that by returning the genuine Hals to the museum we've managed to salvage at least a scrap of Hamilton family honor."

From her place at the perimeter of the main room of the Northern Light exhibition, Paige looked across the crowded gallery to where Anthony Hamilton stood, midway between the serene portrait of "The Lady of Dordrect" and a bevy of television and newspaper reporters. The unflattering glare of their lights drowned out the beauty of the painting's mellow tones and highlighted the lines of creeping dissipation apparent in Anthony's dark face.

"It was really just a mix-up," he was telling the reporters with a forced smile. "My brother, Grant, never knew about the nearly perfect copy of 'The Lady' my father had painted for my mother. He commissioned it years before either of us was born, to hang over the fireplace at Riverview when the original was on extended exhibition elsewhere. There's no comparison between the two paintings when you see them side by side, but the copy was as nearly perfect as the

Portrait of a Lady 175

artist could make it. It's to the credit of Miss Paige Fenton and the staff of the Tri-City Museum that they so quickly discovered that the portrait they were given was not all it seemed. I was out of the country when the news of the forgery broke, but when I realized what had happened, I sent the genuine painting to Chicago to be authenticated, then turned it over to Director Franklin." The reporters scribbled furiously as he spoke, then raised their hands for further questions.

Anthony acknowledged one of them. "Mr. Hamilton, where is the forgery—the copy—of 'The Lady of Dordrect' now, and may we see it?"

Anthony shook his head. "Grant insisted the copy be destroyed immediately to prevent further confusion, and after the fiasco this past week I felt compelled to concur with his decision."

"He's very good at that, isn't he?" Grant inquired quietly as he came up beside Paige. "He has a way of making the most outlandish lies sound like the gospel truth."

It was the first time she'd seen Grant since he'd dropped her off at her apartment that morning after the tense, difficult meeting in Arthur Franklin's office, and she was surprised by the bitterness in his voice. Though he had expressed no opinion about the museum director's decision to avoid more adverse publicity by devising the story Anthony had told the reporters, Paige felt certain Grant wasn't sorry the Hamilton family honor would be preserved and that no criminal charges would be brought against his brother. Though she didn't fully understand the corporate maneuvering, she knew Grant had called a series of emergency meetings at Hamilton Corporation during the afternoon and that Anthony could not have escaped some form of retribution.

Though many things had been resolved in the past hours, Paige still saw pain and disillusionment in Grant's weary eyes. Gently she slipped one arm around his waist and felt him draw her closer in response.

"It's all over, Grant," she comforted him in a whisper.

"What happened with 'The Lady' is behind us now."

His arm tightened around her, and he nuzzled her hair. "I know, Paige. Things have turned out for the best, but I worry about the future."

"You mean you worry about Anthony, don't you?" she murmured.

"Yes, Anthony. I wonder if I'll ever be able to trust him again, or if we'll ever come to terms as I always hoped we could. I want to believe that people change, that time and events can alter what they are."

"I think that's possible, too, but you'll just have to wait and see what happens," she answered philosophically.

He nodded and brushed a kiss against her temple. "I know now what my brother is and what he's capable of doing. Whatever happens, I'll never be so naive in dealing with him again. I always understood what he could do to me, but I never had any inkling of the effect I could have on him."

"Then perhaps you've learned a very important lesson that will help you deal with whatever the future brings."

At her observation his expression softened. "Have I told you in the last ten minutes how much I love you?" he asked her, smiling.

Before she could answer, their conversation was interrupted by Anthony's voice from across the room. "Grant, I've just had a question about the future of the company. I think that, as its newly elected president, you should be the one to answer it."

The announcement caught Paige by surprise, and she barely had time to offer her congratulations before Grant was crossing the gallery with her in tow.

"You see, gentlemen and ladies, I've resigned the presidency of Hamilton Corporation in favor of my brother," Anthony explained. "While he sees to the operations here, I'll be in Europe exploring new markets for our products."

Grant and Paige were in the center of the room, surrounded by reporters and in the glare of their bright lights.

Portrait of a Lady 177

Without fanfare, Anthony Hamilton had stepped aside.

"Mr. Hamilton, what are the plans for the future of Hamilton Corporation?" someone asked.

As Grant skillfully fielded the question, Paige glanced around her at the ring of shadowed faces. She paused to study Anthony. Outside the spotlight now, he was eclipsed by the new power and prestige of his younger brother, as surely and decisively as the earth blocking out the moon. In the moment before he turned to go, Paige saw mirrored in his expression a defeat so devastating and all-encompassing that a wave of selfless pity surged through her. By his deception and deceit he had lost everything, his position at Hamilton Corporation and the power he had sought so ruthlessly, forfeiting it all along with his self-respect. His was the kind of crisis that changed a person, and, for Grant's sake as well as Anthony's, Paige hoped that this experience would make Anthony a better man.

Then her attention turned to Grant once more, strong and sure beside her. His vitality and confidence had never been more evident, and her eyes swept over him with love and pride. The midnight-black tuxedo and white tucked shirt he wore were perfect foils for his tanned, ruddy skin and rich brown hair streaked with gold. The clothes fit him to perfection, outlining the trim, hard lines of his body, and she responded in the same delightful way she had that first night at Arthur Franklin's party. Only now she was sure of him and certain of her own feelings, too, which made the confusion and conflict of these last days seem almost worthwhile.

Paige hadn't been paying attention to the questions Grant was answering, and she was startled when someone directed one to her. "Miss Fenton, do you have anything to add now that the genuine 'The Lady of Dordrect' has been turned over to the museum?"

"Only that I'm glad the mix-up has been resolved and that the painting is part of Tri-City's permanent collection. It's been a trying week for all of us, and since 'The Lady' seems to be content here, we're glad to have her."

A few more voices clamored for recognition, but Grant dismissed them with a wave of his hand. "I think you've asked me quite enough questions about one of my ladies," he told them with a grin, "and now, I have a private question of my own for the other woman in my life."

As the TV lights began to dim, Grant led Paige through the crowded exhibition galleries to the relative quiet of the museum's main hall. He went directly to "their" sculpture and pulled her between two of the huge, sheltering steel plates. Before Paige could say a word, Grant took her face between his palms and kissed her, holding her to his mouth as if she were a delicate snifter of the finest brandy, drinking deeply until they were both intoxicated by their potent emotions.

"I've been waiting all day to do that," he told her as he slid his hands around her back to pull her close.

Paige nestled against him, totally content. "I love you, Grant," she whispered.

"And I love you."

For a moment there seemed nothing more to say as they stood with their arms around each other, secure and serene in their happiness. Then Grant began to fumble in his pockets.

"I have a gift for you," he said as he searched, "and this seems like an appropriate time to present it."

He located what he was seeking in the breast pocket of his jacket. It was a jade ring set with pearls, their pale luminosity enhancing the cool beauty of the round central stone.

"See? I told you the ring was just the color of your eyes," he murmured as he slipped the circlet of gold on the ring finger of her left hand. "I got it from Anthony this afternoon."

"It is just like the one 'The Lady of Dordrect' is wearing."

Grant nodded. "It was my mother's most prized possession, and now I want you to have it."

"Oh, Grant, thank you," Paige breathed as she hugged him. "I don't know what to say."

"You could say that you'll marry me," he suggested with a smile. "If that's what you want, too. I know we haven't known each other very long, but the way I feel about you will last for the rest of our lives. Please, Paige, say you'll marry me."

Looking up into his face, seeing the hard, strong features softened with tenderness and love, Paige gave the only possible answer.

"Yes, I'll marry you, Grant, and I'll always treasure your mother's ring." As she watched it, the stone seemed to glow more brightly, and Paige could almost sense the love and approval of the previous generation of Hamiltons transmitted through the wide, gold band and the smooth, green stone, sanctioning their son's commitment. It was as if the feelings Grant's parents had shared were being passed on through the ring to the two of them.

Grant's blue eyes shone with the promise of their future together as he bent his head to kiss her. "It only seems right that you should have that ring," he commented as his mouth brushed hers, "since it's 'The Lady' who brought us together."

Second Chance at Love

___ 0-425-07977-5	BRIEF ENCOUNTER #252 Aimée Duvall	$2.25
___ 0-425-07978-3	FOREVER EDEN #253 Christa Merlin	$2.25
___ 0-425-07979-1	STARDUST MELODY #254 Mary Haskell	$2.25
___ 0-425-07980-5	HEAVEN TO KISS #255 Charlotte Hines	$2.25
___ 0-425-08014-5	AIN'T MISBEHAVING #256 Jeanne Grant	$2.25
___ 0-425-08015-3	PROMISE ME RAINBOWS #257 Joan Lancaster	$2.25
___ 0-425-08016-1	RITES OF PASSION #258 Jacqueline Topaz	$2.25
___ 0-425-08017-X	ONE IN A MILLION #259 Lee Williams	$2.25
___ 0-425-08018-8	HEART OF GOLD #260 Liz Grady	$2.25
___ 0-425-08019-6	AT LONG LAST LOVE #261 Carole Buck	$2.25
___ 0-425-08150-8	EYE OF THE BEHOLDER #262 Kay Robbins	$2.25
___ 0-425-08151-6	GENTLEMAN AT HEART #263 Elissa Curry	$2.25
___ 0-425-08152-4	BY LOVE POSSESSED #264 Linda Barlow	$2.25
___ 0-425-08153-2	WILDFIRE #265 Kelly Adams	$2.25
___ 0-425-08154-0	PASSION'S DANCE #266 Lauren Fox	$2.25
___ 0-425-08155-9	VENETIAN SUNRISE #267 Kate Nevins	$2.25
___ 0-425-08199-0	THE STEELE TRAP #268 Betsy Osborne	$2.25
___ 0-425-08200-8	LOVE PLAY #269 Carole Buck	$2.25
___ 0-425-08201-6	CAN'T SAY NO #270 Jeanne Grant	$2.25
___ 0-425-08202-4	A LITTLE NIGHT MUSIC #271 Lee Williams	$2.25
___ 0-425-08203-2	A BIT OF DARING #272 Mary Haskell	$2.25
___ 0-425-08204-0	THIEF OF HEARTS #273 Jan Mathews	$2.25
___ 0-425-08284-9	MASTER TOUCH #274 Jasmine Craig	$2.25
___ 0-425-08285-7	NIGHT OF A THOUSAND STARS #275 Petra Diamond	$2.25
___ 0-425-08286-5	UNDERCOVER KISSES #276 Laine Allen	$2.25
___ 0-425-08287-3	MAN TROUBLE #277 Elizabeth Henry	$2.25
___ 0-425-08288-1	SUDDENLY THAT SUMMER #278 Jennifer Rose	$2.25
___ 0-425-08289-X	SWEET ENCHANTMENT #279 Diana Mars	$2.25
___ 0-425-08461-2	SUCH ROUGH SPLENDOR #280 Cinda Richards	$2.25
___ 0-425-08462-0	WINDFLAME #281 Sarah Crewe	$2.25
___ 0-425-08463-9	STORM AND STARLIGHT #282 Lauren Fox	$2.25
___ 0-425-08464-7	HEART OF THE HUNTER #283 Liz Grady	$2.25
___ 0-425-08465-5	LUCKY'S WOMAN #284 Delaney Devers	$2.25
___ 0-425-08466-3	PORTRAIT OF A LADY #285 Elizabeth N. Kary	$2.25

Prices may be slightly higher in Canada.

Available at your local bookstore or return this form to:

SECOND CHANCE AT LOVE
Book Mailing Service
P.O. Box 690, Rockville Centre, NY 11571

Please send me the titles checked above. I enclose _____ Include 75¢ for postage and handling if one book is ordered; 25¢ per book for two or more not to exceed $1.75. California, Illinois, New York and Tennessee residents please add sales tax.

NAME_____

ADDRESS_____

CITY_____ STATE/ZIP_____

(allow six weeks for delivery)

SK-41b

COMING NEXT MONTH IN THE SECOND CHANCE AT LOVE SERIES

ANYTHING GOES #286 by Diana Morgan
Zany inventor Kyle Bennett challenges Angie Carpenter's title as Supermom by waging a housekeeping competition with his robot...then sweeping Angie off her feet!

SOPHISTICATED LADY #287 by Elissa Curry
Despite her highfalutin name and prim good looks, Abigail Vanderbine has trouble controlling her all-too-natural impulses around wholesomely sexy peanut-butter manufacturer Mick Piper!

THE PHOENIX HEART #288 by Betsy Osborne
Nothing's quite proper in Alyssa Courtney's proper life once laid-back cartoonist Rade Stone showers her with gifts and advice...then transforms her into a shameless wanton!

FALLEN ANGEL #289 by Carole Buck
Rock star Mallory Victor, floundering in a glitzy, ephemeral world, yearns to trade the limelight for a love life with rock-solid David Hitchcock, the man she's sure can save her.

THE SWEETHEART TRUST #290 by Hilary Cole
Collaborating with writer Nick Trent becomes infinitely complicated when Kate Fairchild inherits a crumbling Victorian mansion...and seizes the chance to domesticate Nick into the man of her dreams.

DEAR HEART #291 by Lee Williams
Charly Lynn thinks no *real* man is as sensitive as Robert Heart, her favorite lovelorn columnist. Certainly not Bret Roberts, with his devilish chimpanzee and presumptuous come-ons!

QUESTIONNAIRE

1. How do you rate _____
   (please print TITLE)
   - ☐ excellent
   - ☐ good
   - ☐ very good
   - ☐ fair
   - ☐ poor

2. How likely are you to purchase another book in this series?
   - ☐ definitely would purchase
   - ☐ probably would purchase
   - ☐ probably would not purchase
   - ☐ definitely would not purchase

3. How likely are you to purchase another book by this author?
   - ☐ definitely would purchase
   - ☐ probably would purchase
   - ☐ probably would not purchase
   - ☐ definitely would not purchase

4. How does this book compare to books in other contemporary romance lines?
   - ☐ much better
   - ☐ better
   - ☐ about the same
   - ☐ not as good
   - ☐ definitely not as good

5. Why did you buy this book? (Check as many as apply)
   - ☐ I have read other SECOND CHANCE AT LOVE romances
   - ☐ friend's recommendation
   - ☐ bookseller's recommendation
   - ☐ art on the front cover
   - ☐ description of the plot on the back cover
   - ☐ book review I read
   - ☐ other _____

(Continued...)

6. Please list your three favorite contemporary romance lines.
   _____
   _____

7. Please list your favorite authors of contemporary romance lines.
   _____
   _____
   _____
   _____
   _____

8. How many SECOND CHANCE AT LOVE romances have you read? _____

9. How many series romances like SECOND CHANCE AT LOVE do you <u>read</u> each month? _____

10. How many series romances like SECOND CHANCE AT LOVE do you <u>buy</u> each month? _____

11. Mind telling your age?
    ☐ under 18
    ☐ 18 to 30
    ☐ 31 to 45
    ☐ over 45

☐ Please check if you'd like to receive our <u>free</u> SECOND CHANCE AT LOVE Newsletter.

We hope you'll share your other ideas about romances with us on an additional sheet and attach it securely to this questionnaire.

• •

Fill in your name and address below:
Name _____
Street Address _____
City _____ State _____ Zip _____

Please return this questionnaire to:
   SECOND CHANCE AT LOVE
   The Berkley Publishing Group
   200 Madison Avenue, New York, New York 10016